CARTOON NETWORK

BEN 10

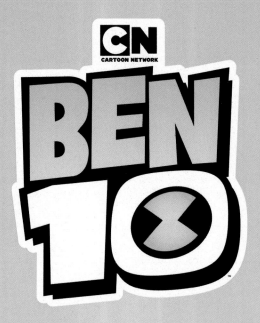

MECHA MADNESS

kaboom!

Ross Richie CEO & Founder
Joy Huffman CFO
Matt Gagnon Editor-in-Chief
Filip Sablik President, Publishing & Marketing
Stephen Christy President, Development
Lance Kreiter Vice President, Licensing & Merchandising
Arune Singh Vice President, Marketing
Bryce Carlson Vice President, Editorial & Creative Strategy
Scott Newman Manager, Production Design
Kate Henning Manager, Operations
Spencer Simpson Manager, Sales
Elyse Strandberg Manager, Finance
Sierra Hahn Executive Editor
Jeanine Schaefer Executive Editor
Dafna Pleban Senior Editor
Shannon Watters Senior Editor
Eric Harburn Senior Editor
Chris Rosa Editor
Matthew Levine Editor
Sophie Philips-Roberts Associate Editor
Amanda LaFranco Associate Editor
Gavin Gronenthal Assistant Editor
Gwen Waller Assistant Editor
Allyson Gronowitz Assistant Editor
Jillian Crab Design Coordinator
Michelle Ankley Design Coordinator
Kara Leopard Production Designer
Marie Krupina Production Designer
Grace Park Production Designer
Chelsea Roberts Production Design Assistant
Samantha Knapp Production Design Assistant
Paola Capalla Senior Accountant
José Meza Live Events Lead
Stephanie Hocutt Digital Marketing Lead
Esther Kim Marketing Coordinator
Cat O'Grady Digital Marketing Coordinator
Amanda Lawson Marketing Assistant
Holly Aitchison Digital Sales Coordinator
Morgan Perry Retail Sales Coordinator
Megan Christopher Operations Coordinator
Rodrigo Hernandez Mailroom Assistant
Zipporah Smith Operations Assistant
Breanna Sarpy Executive Assistant

For information regarding the CPSIA on this printed material, call: (203) 595-3636 and provide reference #RICH – 865881.

BOOM! Studios, 5670 Wilshire Boulevard, Suite 400, Los Angeles, CA 90036-5679.

Printed in USA. First Printing.

ISBN: 978-1-68415-420-3
eISBN: 978-1-64144-537-5

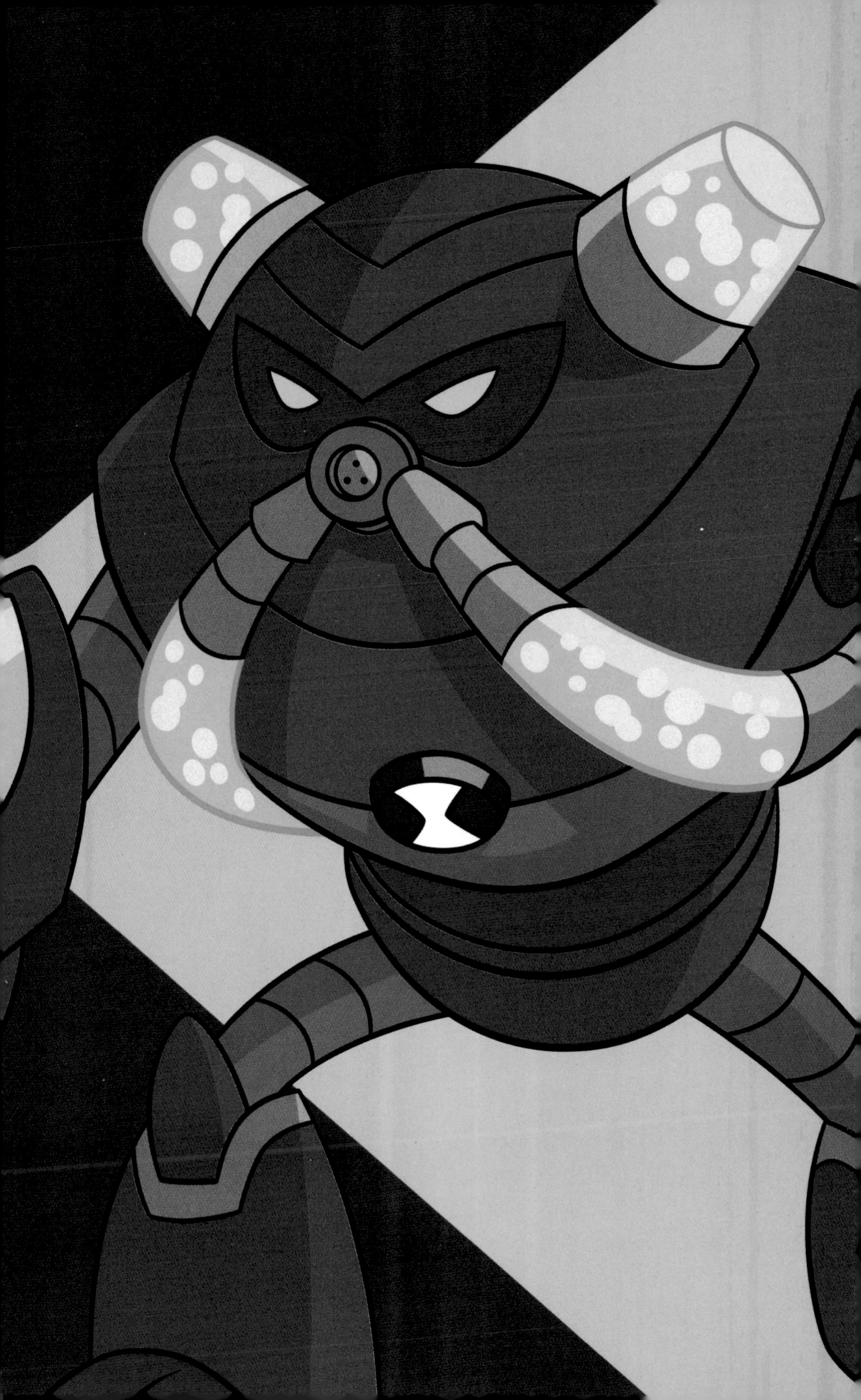

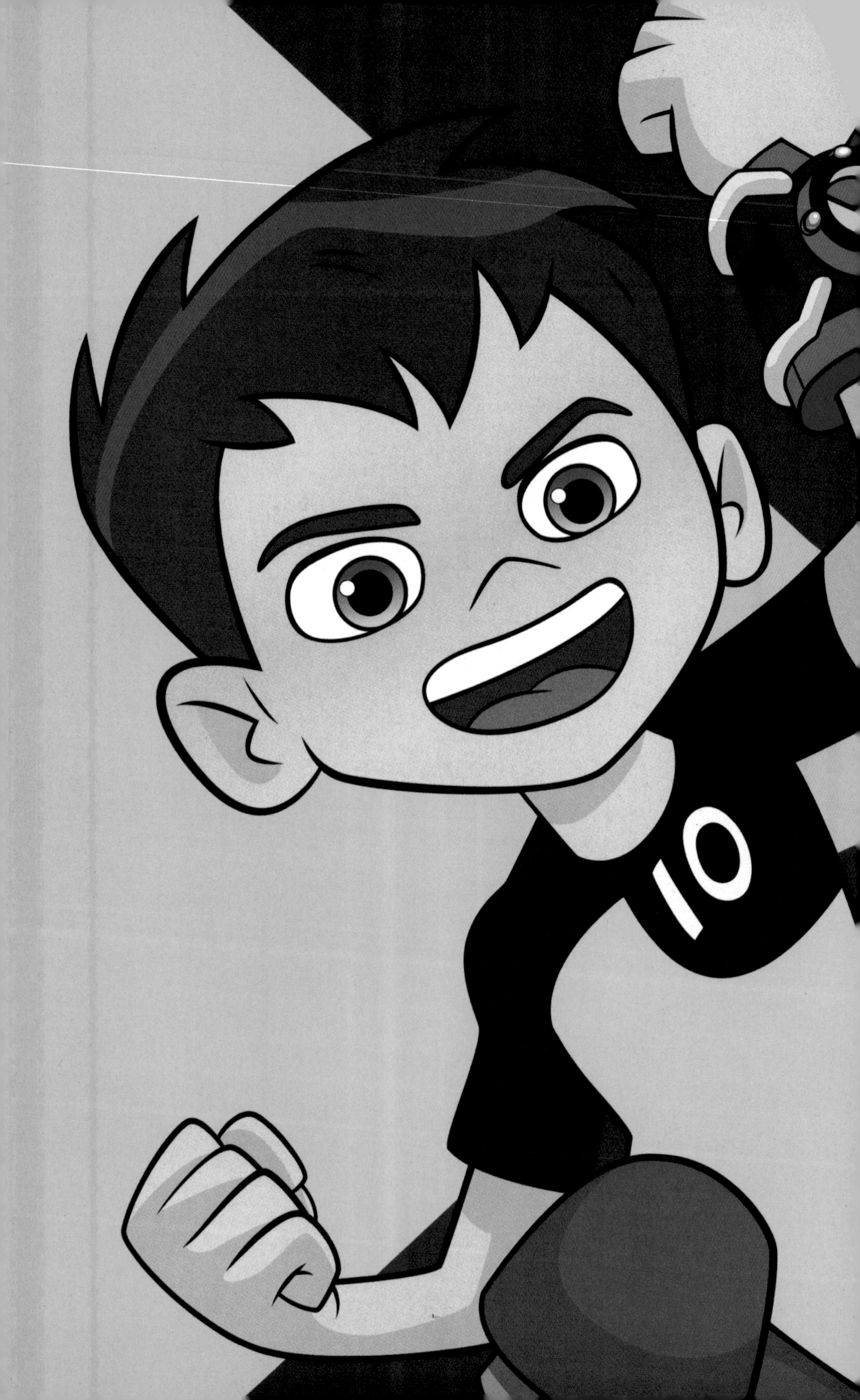
10

BEN TENNYSON IN...

MECHA MADNESS

CREATED BY
MAN OF ACTION

WRITTEN BY
C.B. LEE

ILLUSTRATED BY
LIDAN CHEN

COLORED BY
ELEONORA BRUNI

LETTERED BY
WARREN MONTGOMERY

COVER BY
MATTIA DI MEO

DESIGNER
JILLIAN CRAB

ASSISTANT EDITOR
MICHAEL MOCCIO

EDITOR
MATTHEW LEVINE

WITH SPECIAL THANKS TO
**MARISA MARIONAKIS, JANET NO,
AUSTIN PAGE, TRAMM WIGZELL,
KEITH FAY, SHAREENA CARLSON,**
AND THE WONDERFUL FOLKS AT
CARTOON NETWORK.

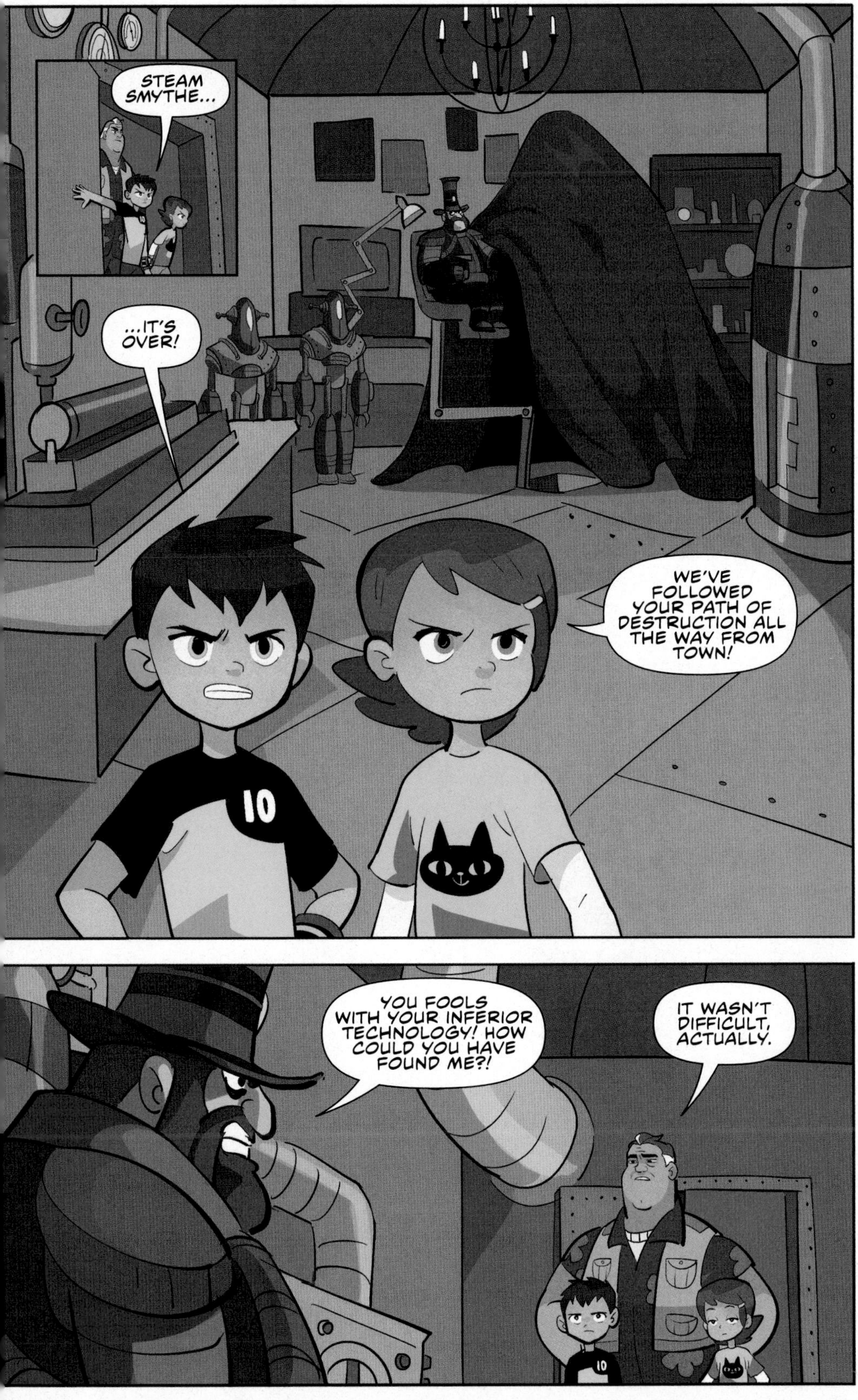
STEAM SMYTHE...
...IT'S OVER!
WE'VE FOLLOWED YOUR PATH OF DESTRUCTION ALL THE WAY FROM TOWN!
10
YOU FOOLS WITH YOUR INFERIOR TECHNOLOGY! HOW COULD YOU HAVE FOUND ME?!
IT WASN'T DIFFICULT, ACTUALLY.

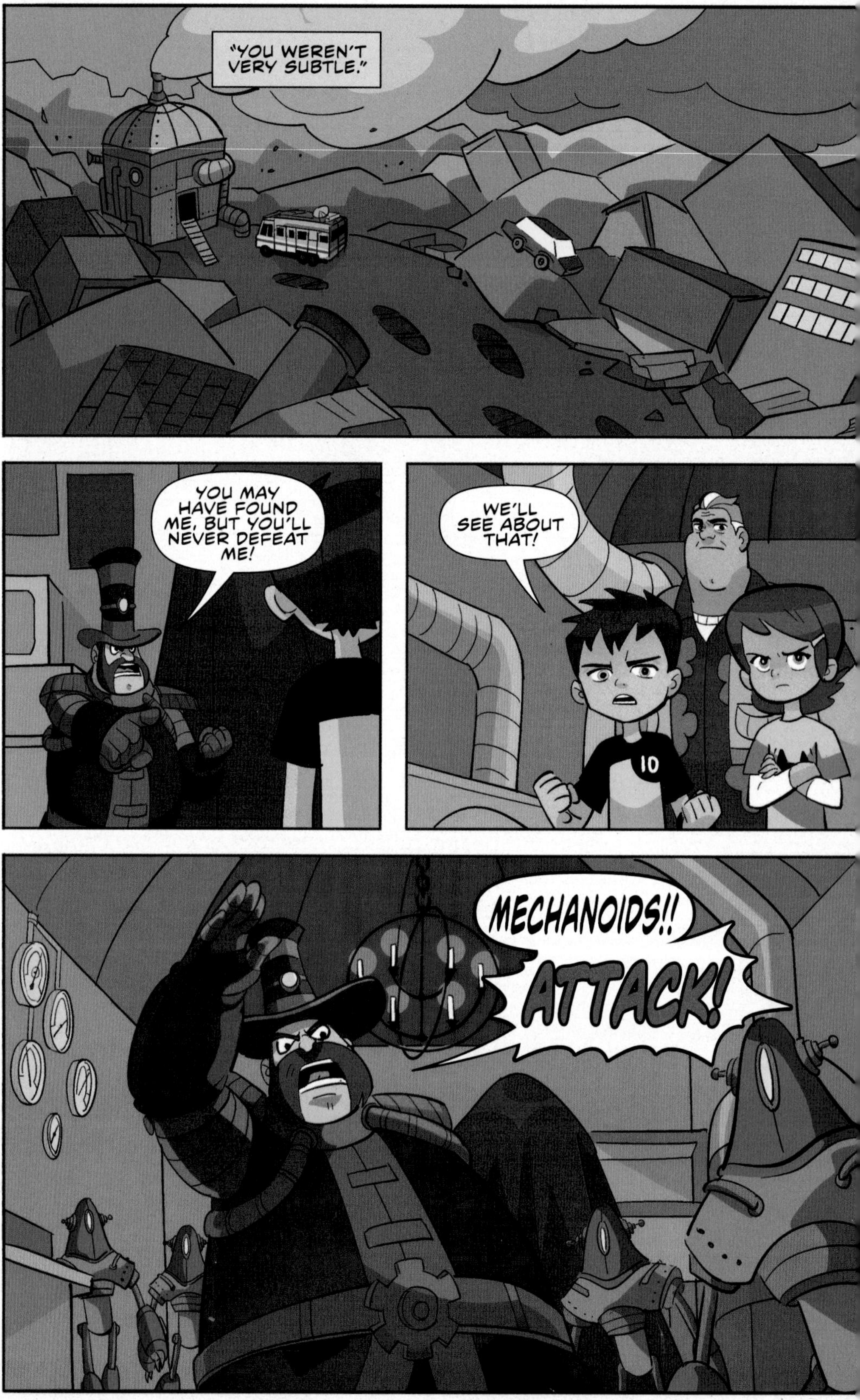
"YOU WEREN'T VERY SUBTLE."
YOU MAY HAVE FOUND ME, BUT YOU'LL NEVER DEFEAT ME!
WE'LL SEE ABOUT THAT!
10
MECHANOIDS!!
ATTACK!

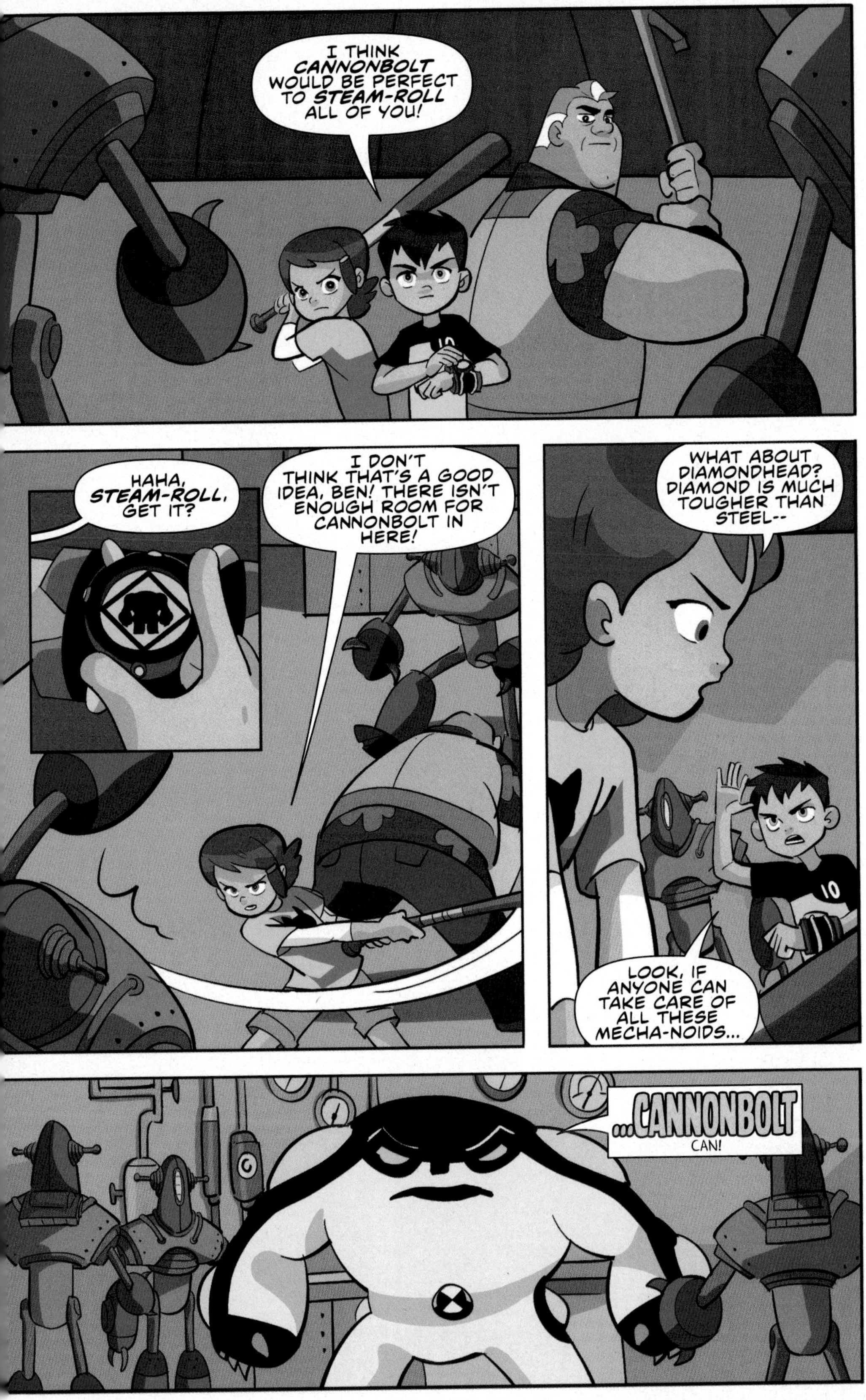
I THINK CANNONBOLT WOULD BE PERFECT TO STEAM-ROLL ALL OF YOU!
HAHA, STEAM-ROLL, GET IT?
I DON'T THINK THAT'S A GOOD IDEA, BEN! THERE ISN'T ENOUGH ROOM FOR CANNONBOLT IN HERE!
WHAT ABOUT DIAMONDHEAD? DIAMOND IS MUCH TOUGHER THAN STEEL--
LOOK, IF ANYONE CAN TAKE CARE OF ALL THESE MECHA-NOIDS...
...CANNONBOLT CAN!

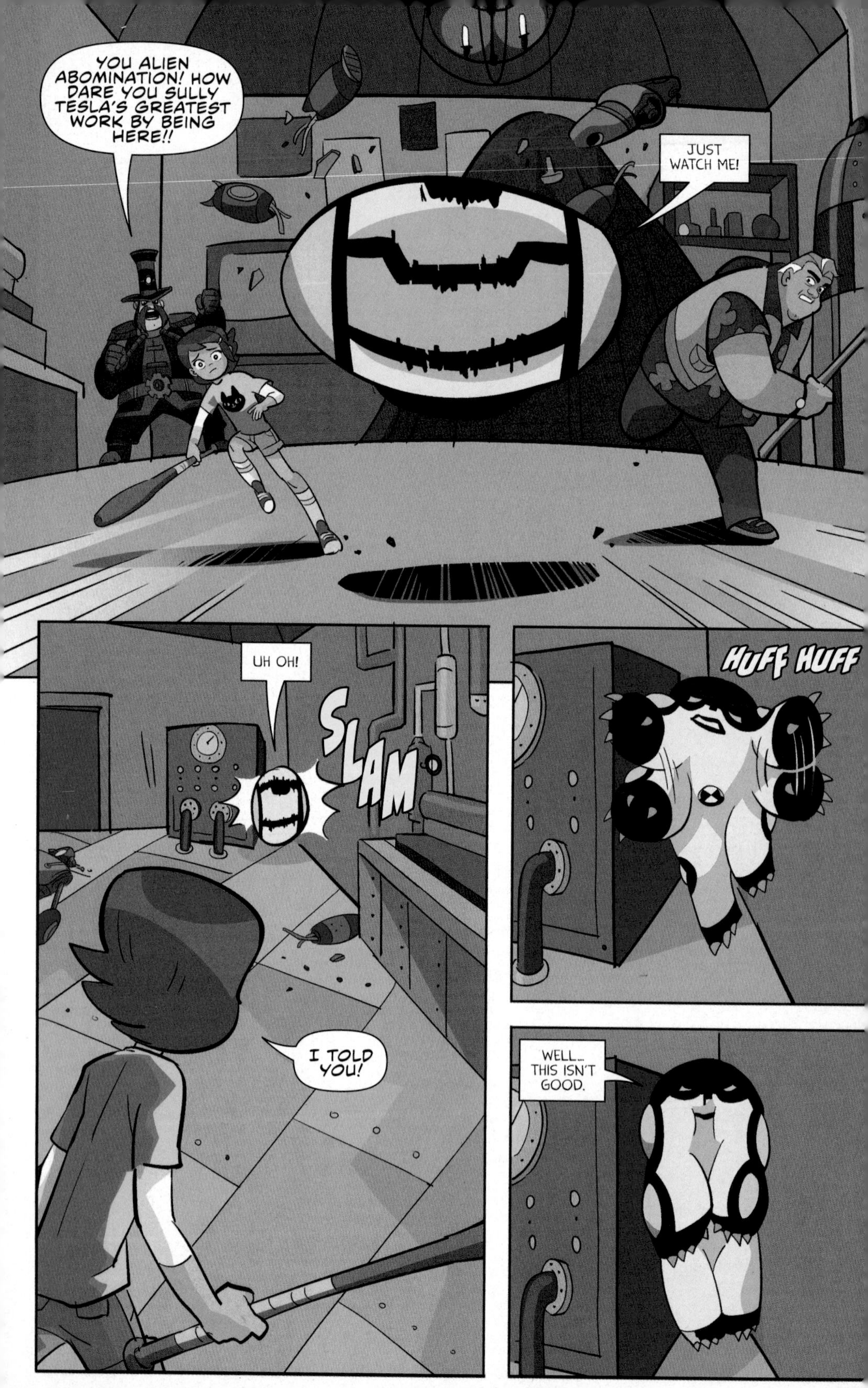
YOU ALIEN ABOMINATION! HOW DARE YOU SULLY TESLA'S GREATEST WORK BY BEING HERE!!
JUST WATCH ME!
UH OH!
SLAM
I TOLD YOU!
HUFF HUFF
WELL... THIS ISN'T GOOD.

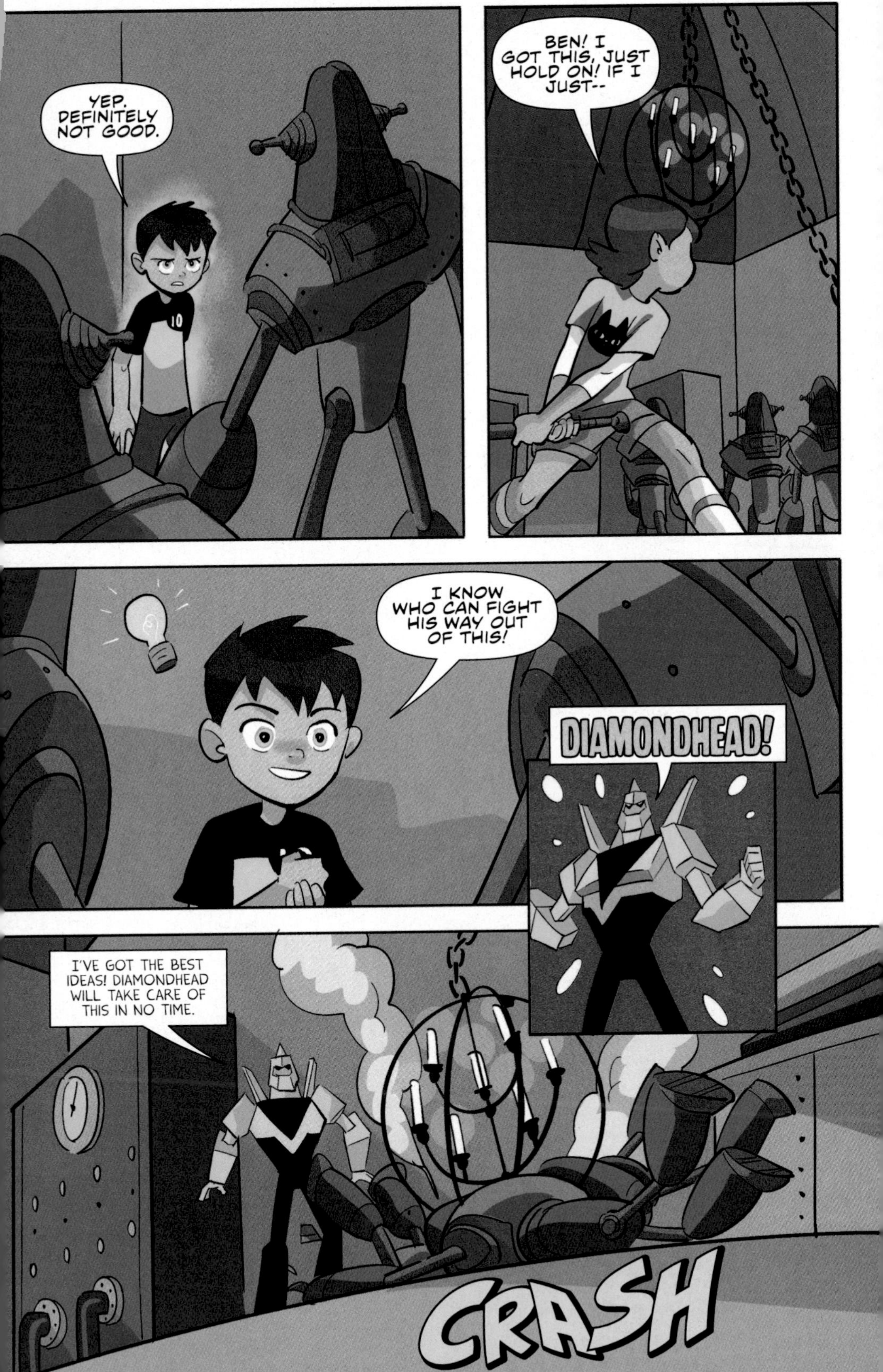
YEP. DEFINITELY NOT GOOD.
BEN! I GOT THIS, JUST HOLD ON! IF I JUST--
I KNOW WHO CAN FIGHT HIS WAY OUT OF THIS!
DIAMONDHEAD!
I'VE GOT THE BEST IDEAS! DIAMONDHEAD WILL TAKE CARE OF THIS IN NO TIME.
CRASH

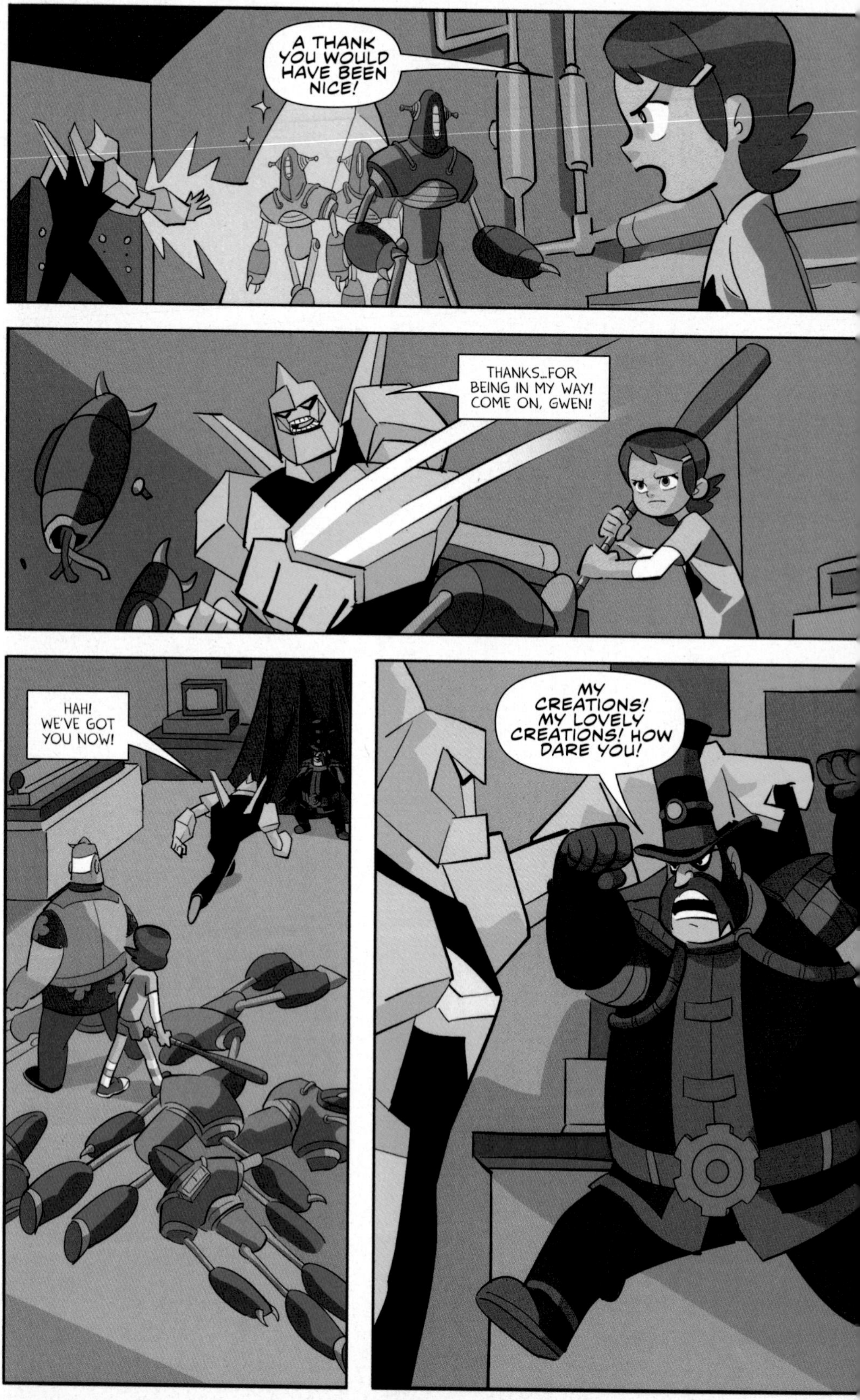
A THANK YOU WOULD HAVE BEEN NICE!
THANKS...FOR BEING IN MY WAY! COME ON, GWEN!
HAH! WE'VE GOT YOU NOW!
MY CREATIONS! MY LOVELY CREATIONS! HOW DARE YOU!

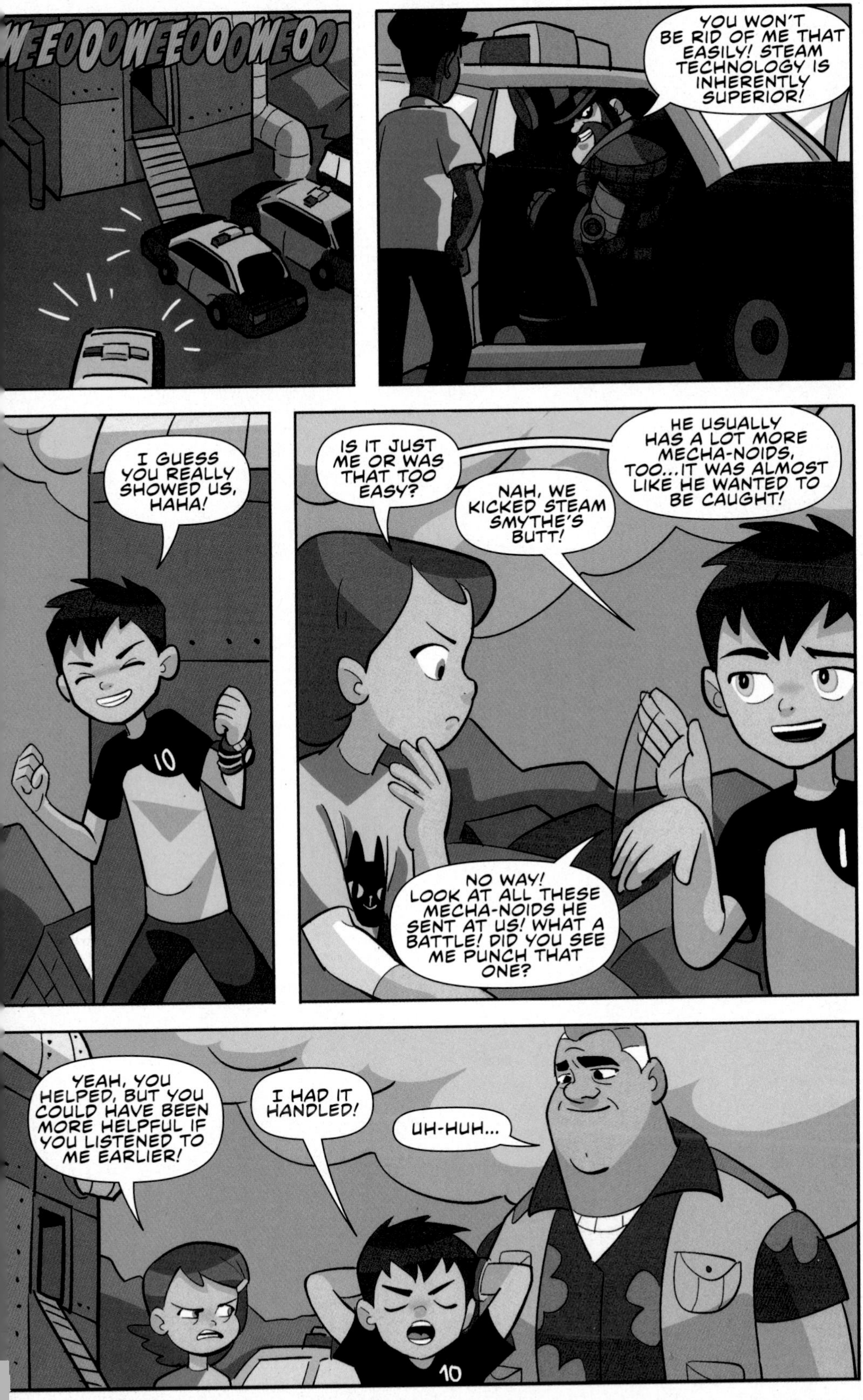
WEEOOOWEEOOOWEOO
YOU WON'T BE RID OF ME THAT EASILY! STEAM TECHNOLOGY IS INHERENTLY SUPERIOR!
I GUESS YOU REALLY SHOWED US, HAHA!
IS IT JUST ME OR WAS THAT TOO EASY?
NAH, WE KICKED STEAM SMYTHE'S BUTT!
HE USUALLY HAS A LOT MORE MECHA-NOIDS, TOO...IT WAS ALMOST LIKE HE WANTED TO BE CAUGHT!
NO WAY! LOOK AT ALL THESE MECHA-NOIDS HE SENT AT US! WHAT A BATTLE! DID YOU SEE ME PUNCH THAT ONE?
YEAH, YOU HELPED, BUT YOU COULD HAVE BEEN MORE HELPFUL IF YOU LISTENED TO ME EARLIER!
I HAD IT HANDLED!
UH-HUH...

I WONDER IF WE CAN FIND ANY CLUES ABOUT WHAT HE WAS UP TO...

GOOD CALL. I DON'T LIKE THE WAY HE SEEMED TO JUST GIVE UP.

HAHA, LOOK HOW "SUPERIOR" THIS TECHNOLOGY IS!

WHAT'S THIS?

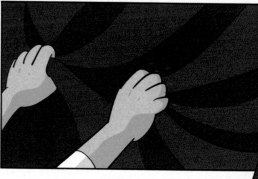

FWOOSH

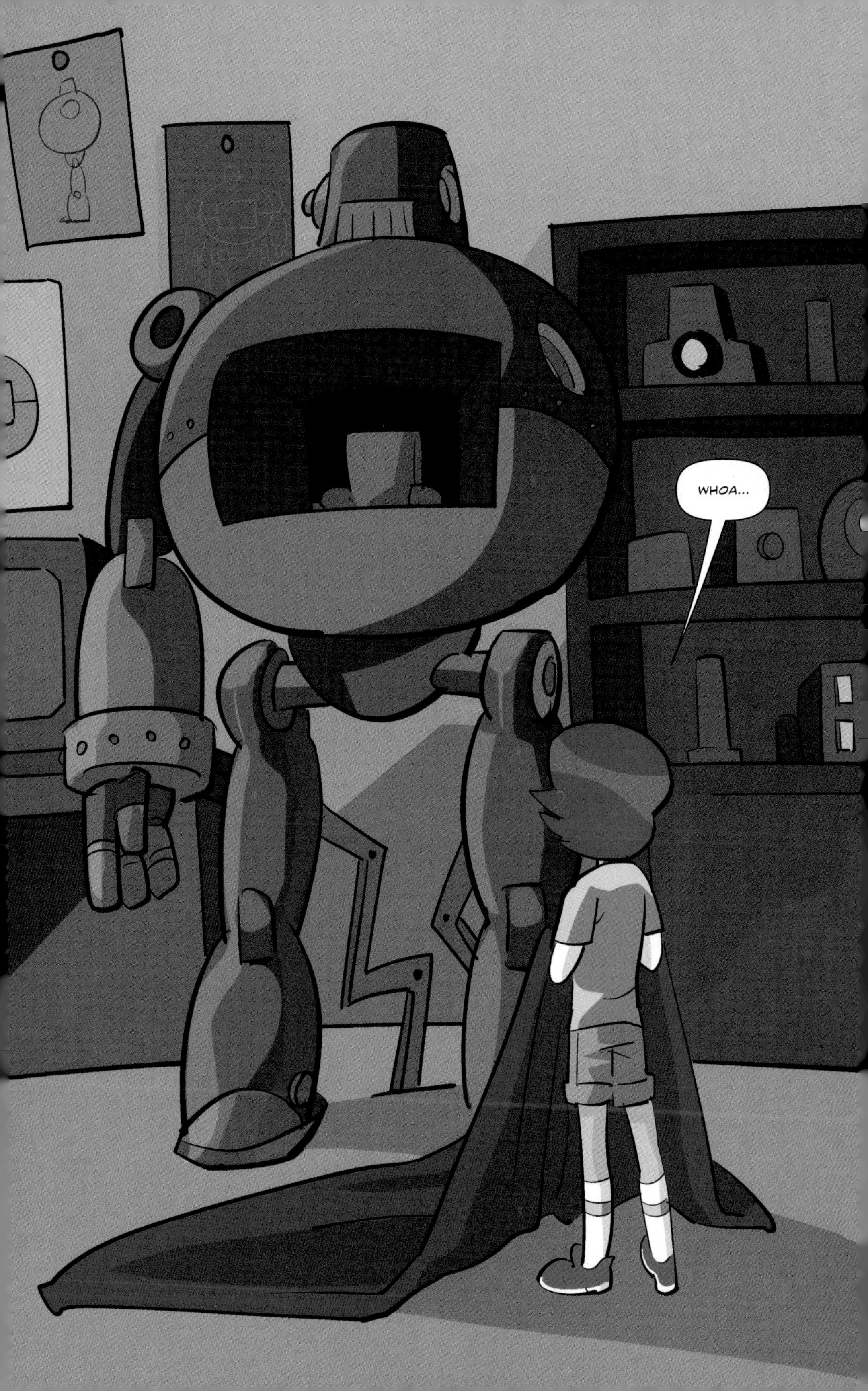
WHOA...

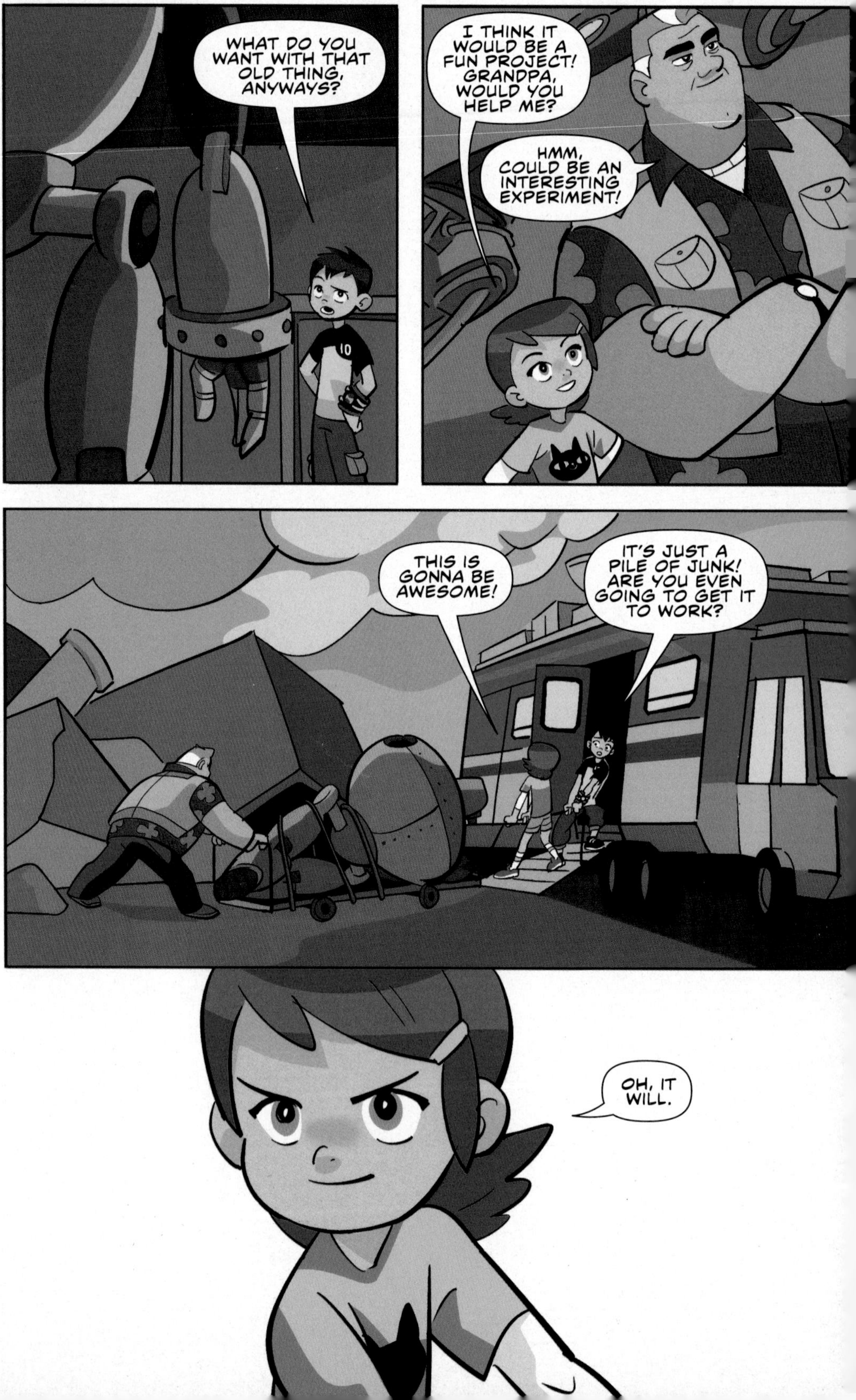
WHAT DO YOU WANT WITH THAT OLD THING, ANYWAYS?
I THINK IT WOULD BE A FUN PROJECT! GRANDPA, WOULD YOU HELP ME?
HMM, COULD BE AN INTERESTING EXPERIMENT!
THIS IS GONNA BE AWESOME!
IT'S JUST A PILE OF JUNK! ARE YOU EVEN GOING TO GET IT TO WORK?
OH, IT WILL.

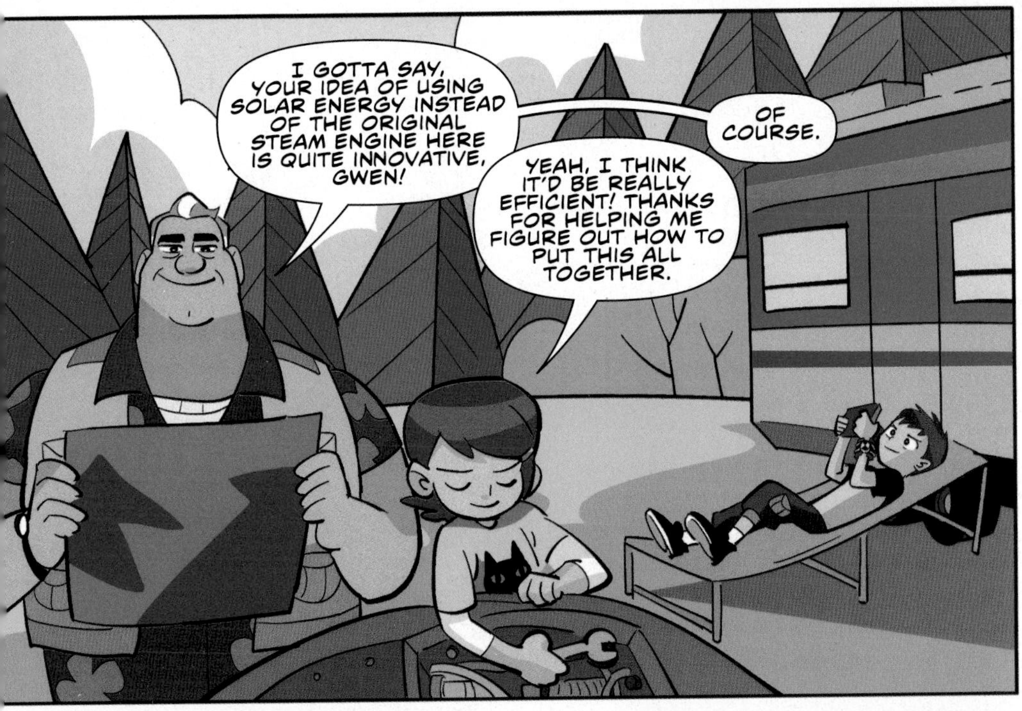
I GOTTA SAY, YOUR IDEA OF USING SOLAR ENERGY INSTEAD OF THE ORIGINAL STEAM ENGINE HERE IS QUITE INNOVATIVE, GWEN!
OF COURSE.
YEAH, I THINK IT'D BE REALLY EFFICIENT! THANKS FOR HELPING ME FIGURE OUT HOW TO PUT THIS ALL TOGETHER.

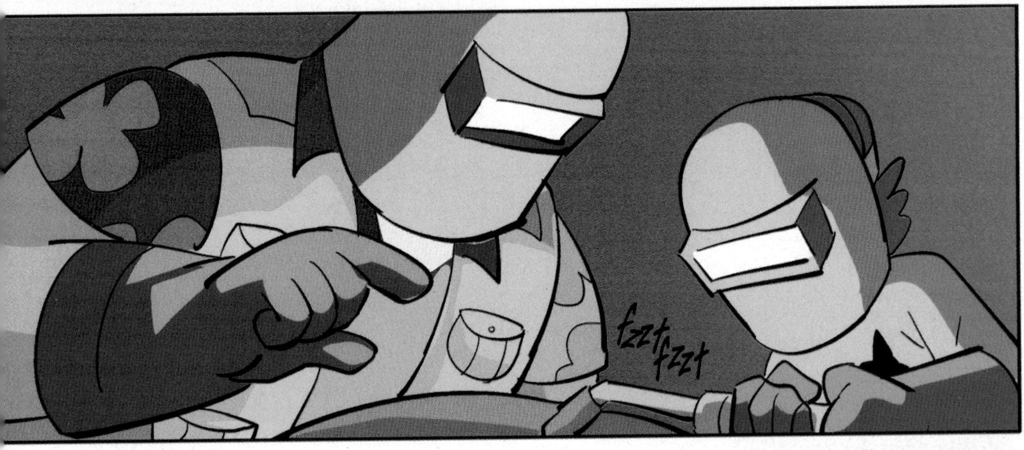
fzzt fzzt

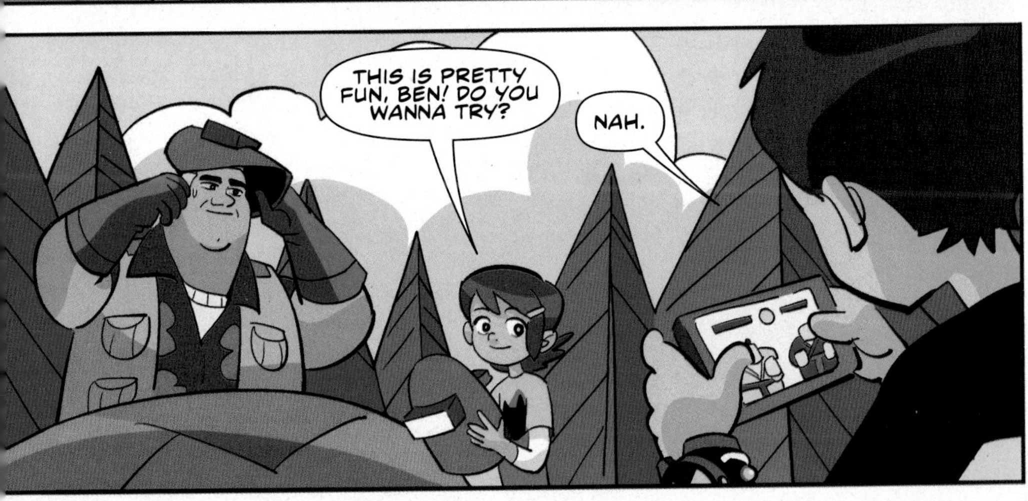
THIS IS PRETTY FUN, BEN! DO YOU WANNA TRY?
NAH.

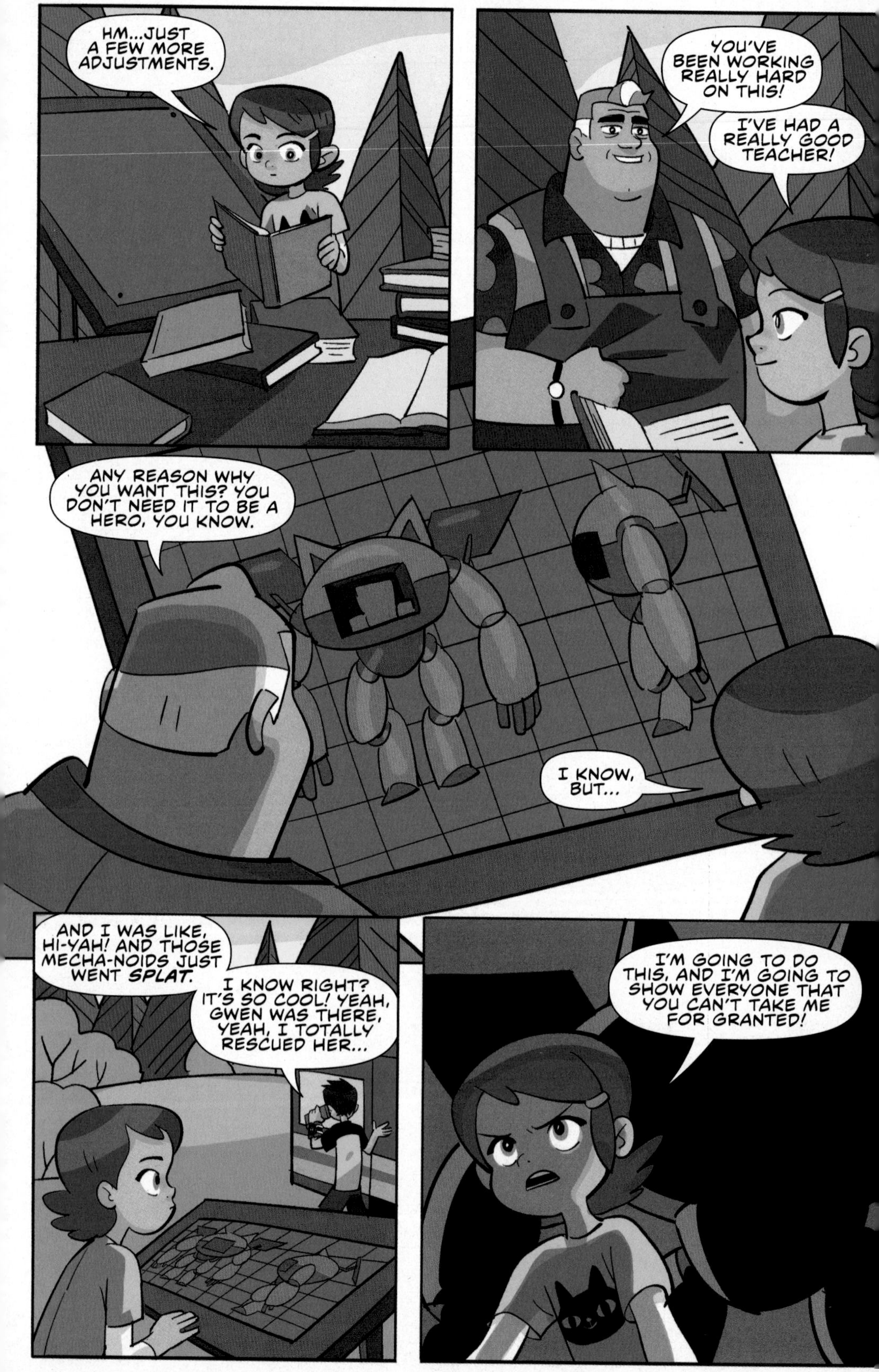
HM...JUST A FEW MORE ADJUSTMENTS.
YOU'VE BEEN WORKING REALLY HARD ON THIS!
I'VE HAD A REALLY GOOD TEACHER!
ANY REASON WHY YOU WANT THIS? YOU DON'T NEED IT TO BE A HERO, YOU KNOW.
I KNOW, BUT...
AND I WAS LIKE, HI-YAH! AND THOSE MECHA-NOIDS JUST WENT SPLAT.
I KNOW RIGHT? IT'S SO COOL! YEAH, GWEN WAS THERE, YEAH, I TOTALLY RESCUED HER...
I'M GOING TO DO THIS, AND I'M GOING TO SHOW EVERYONE THAT YOU CAN'T TAKE ME FOR GRANTED!

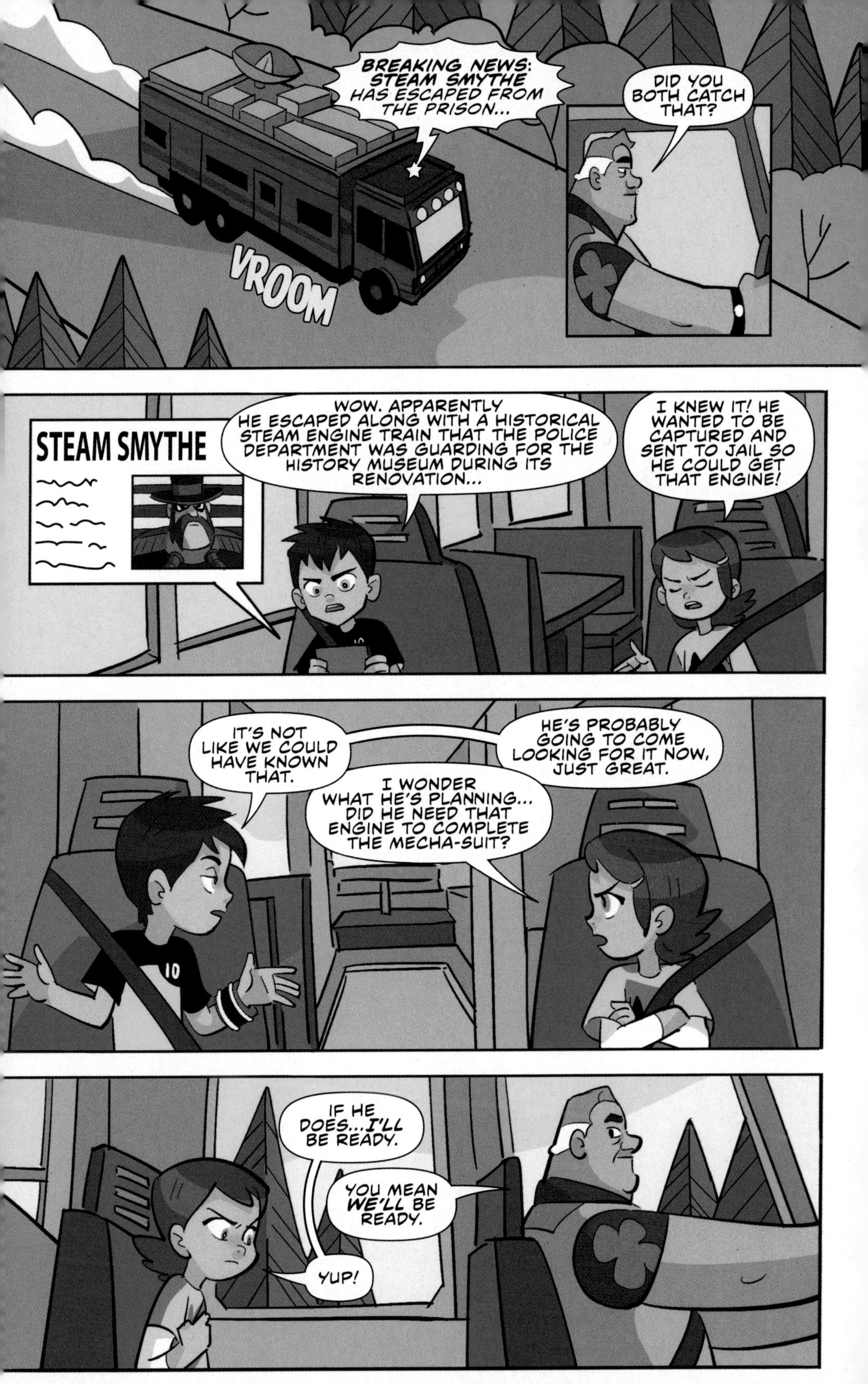

BREAKING NEWS: STEAM SMYTHE HAS ESCAPED FROM THE PRISON...
VROOM
DID YOU BOTH CATCH THAT?
STEAM SMYTHE
WOW. APPARENTLY HE ESCAPED ALONG WITH A HISTORICAL STEAM ENGINE TRAIN THAT THE POLICE DEPARTMENT WAS GUARDING FOR THE HISTORY MUSEUM DURING ITS RENOVATION...
I KNEW IT! HE WANTED TO BE CAPTURED AND SENT TO JAIL SO HE COULD GET THAT ENGINE!
IT'S NOT LIKE WE COULD HAVE KNOWN THAT.
HE'S PROBABLY GOING TO COME LOOKING FOR IT NOW, JUST GREAT.
I WONDER WHAT HE'S PLANNING... DID HE NEED THAT ENGINE TO COMPLETE THE MECHA-SUIT?
IF HE DOES... I'LL BE READY.
YOU MEAN WE'LL BE READY.
YUP!

I CAN'T BELIEVE THIS...WITH THAT ENGINE I STOLE, I HAVE ALL THIS POWER AT MY DISPOSAL AND MY BELOVED NEW CREATION IS JUST *GONE!*

HAHAHAHA! YOU AREN'T AS ELEGANT AS MY ORIGINAL DESIGN, BUT I DARESAY YOU'LL GET THE JOB DONE, MY *MECHA-HAWK!*

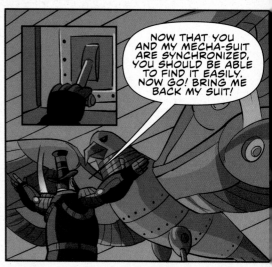

NOW THAT YOU AND MY MECHA-SUIT ARE SYNCHRONIZED, YOU SHOULD BE ABLE TO FIND IT EASILY. NOW GO! BRING ME BACK MY SUIT!

CAW!

AND IF YOU DESTROY ANY INFERIOR TECHNOLOGY ALONG THE WAY, ALL THE BETTER!

CAW! CAW!

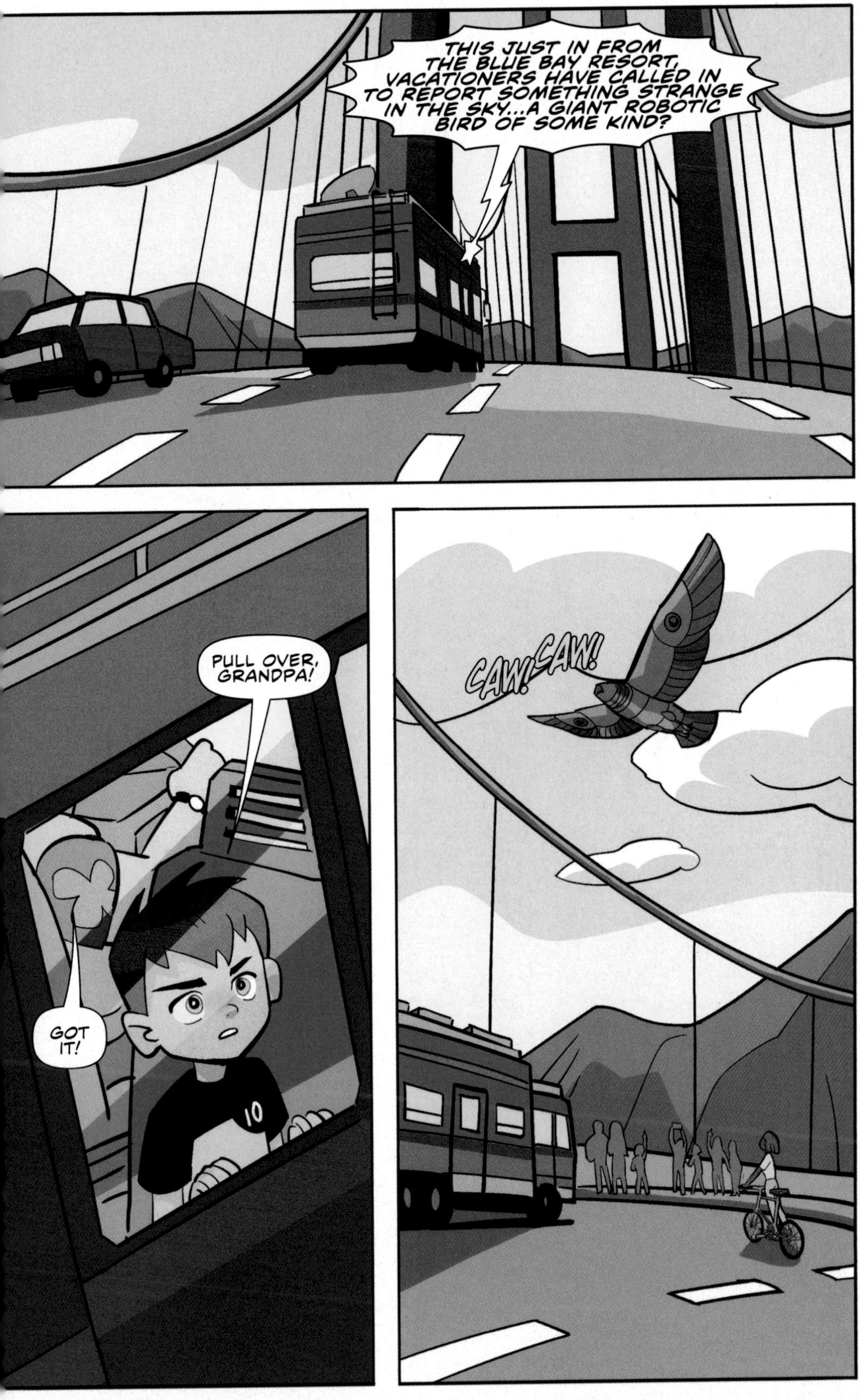
THIS JUST IN FROM THE BLUE BAY RESORT, VACATIONERS HAVE CALLED IN TO REPORT SOMETHING STRANGE IN THE SKY...A GIANT ROBOTIC BIRD OF SOME KIND?
PULL OVER, GRANDPA!
GOT IT!
CAW! CAW!

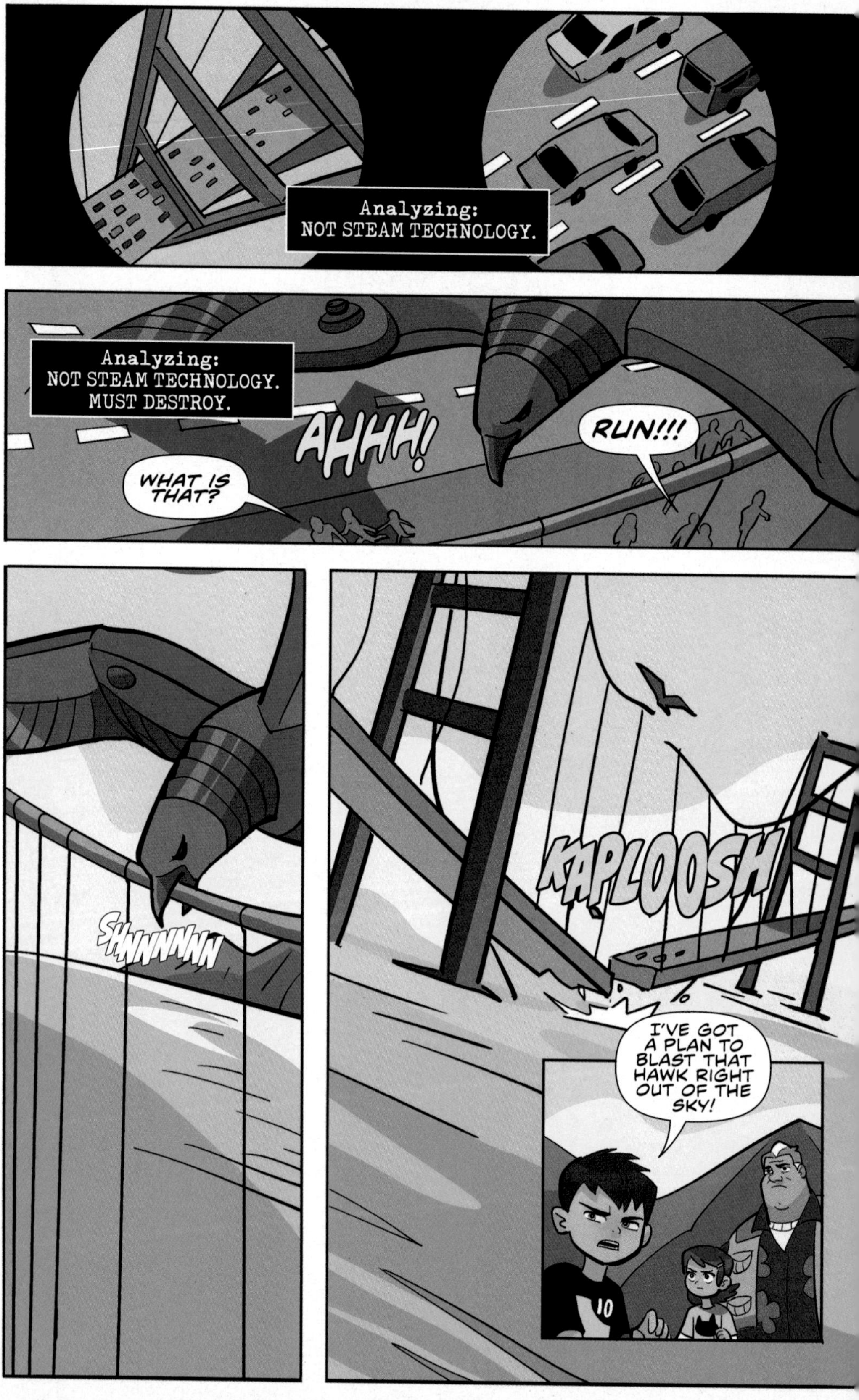
Analyzing:
NOT STEAM TECHNOLOGY.
Analyzing:
NOT STEAM TECHNOLOGY.
MUST DESTROY.
AHHH!
WHAT IS THAT?
RUN!!!
SHNNNNNN
KAPLOOSH
I'VE GOT A PLAN TO BLAST THAT HAWK RIGHT OUT OF THE SKY!
10

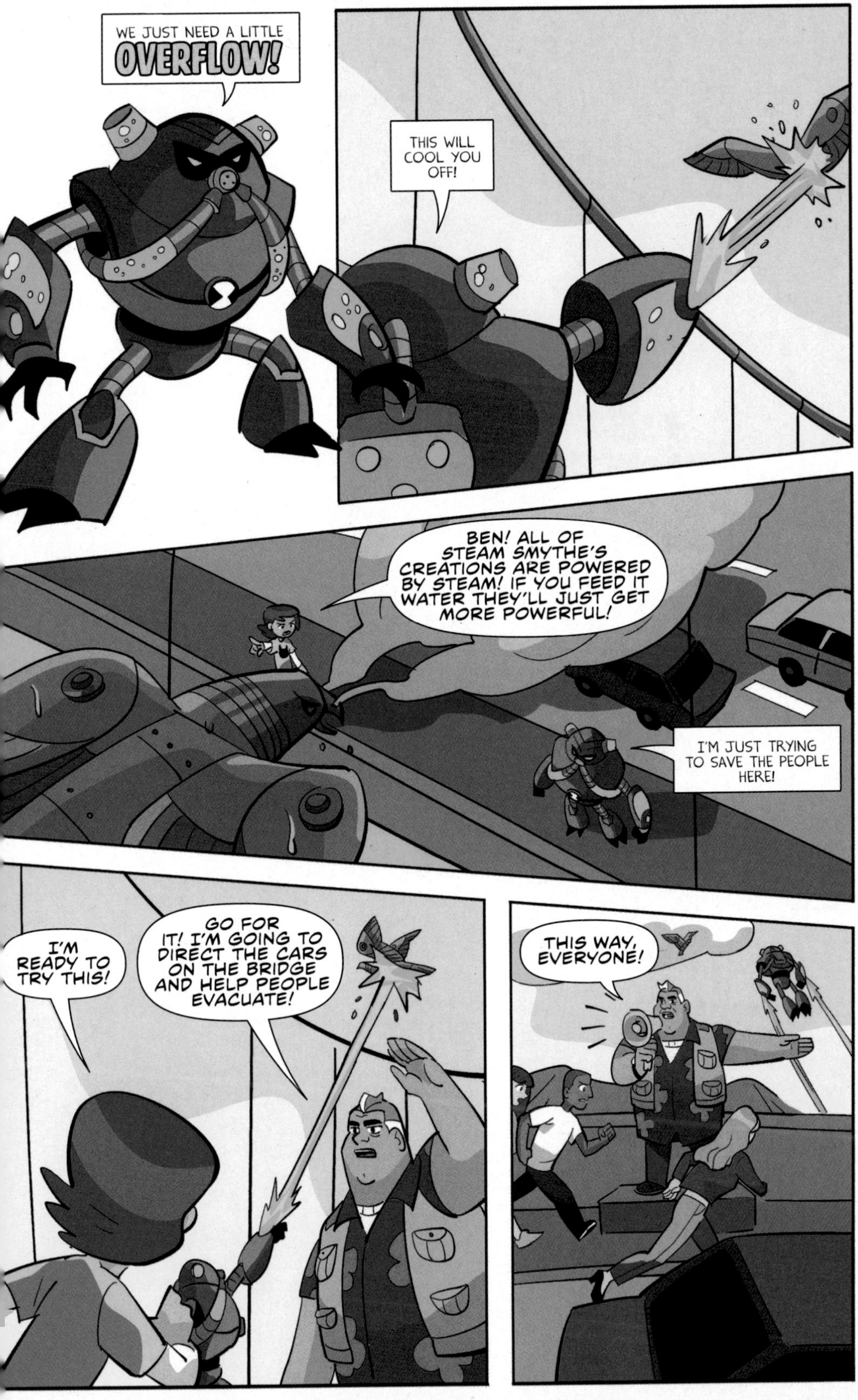
WE JUST NEED A LITTLE OVERFLOW!
THIS WILL COOL YOU OFF!
BEN! ALL OF STEAM SMYTHE'S CREATIONS ARE POWERED BY STEAM! IF YOU FEED IT WATER THEY'LL JUST GET MORE POWERFUL!
I'M JUST TRYING TO SAVE THE PEOPLE HERE!
I'M READY TO TRY THIS!
GO FOR IT! I'M GOING TO DIRECT THE CARS ON THE BRIDGE AND HELP PEOPLE EVACUATE!
THIS WAY, EVERYONE!

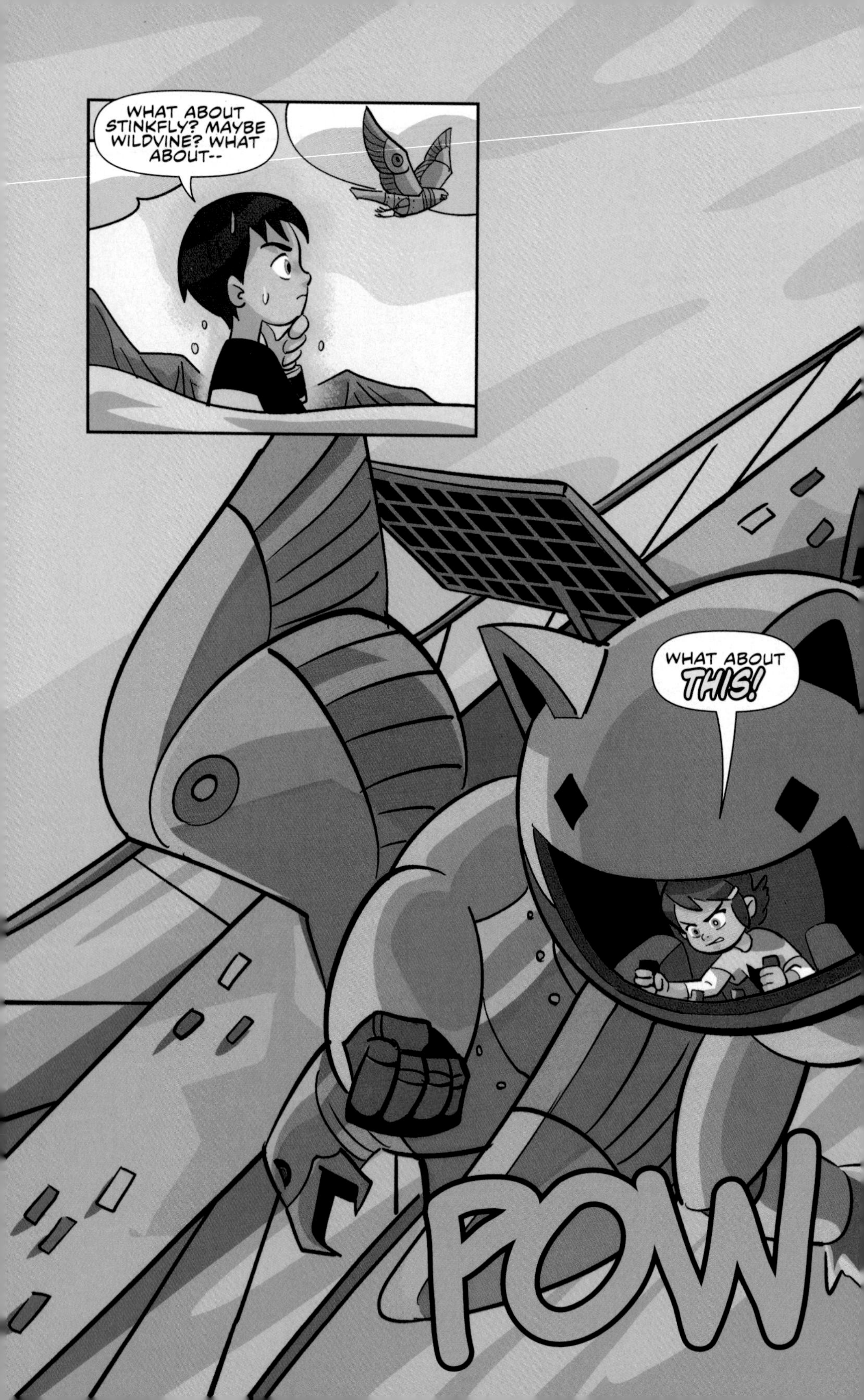
WHAT ABOUT STINKFLY? MAYBE WILDVINE? WHAT ABOUT--
WHAT ABOUT THIS!
POW

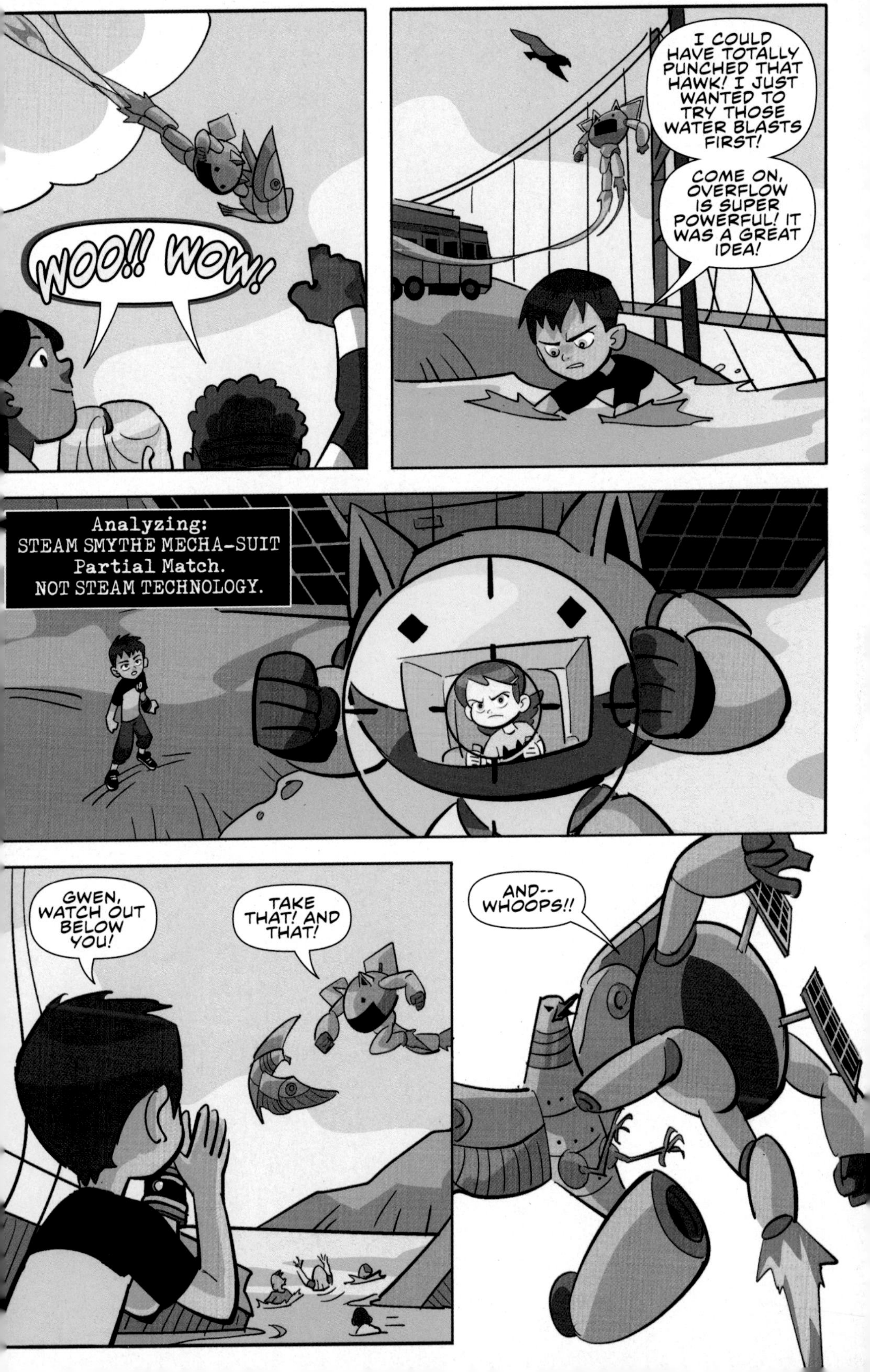
WOO!! WOW!
I COULD HAVE TOTALLY PUNCHED THAT HAWK! I JUST WANTED TO TRY THOSE WATER BLASTS FIRST!
COME ON, OVERFLOW IS SUPER POWERFUL! IT WAS A GREAT IDEA!
Analyzing:
STEAM SMYTHE MECHA-SUIT
Partial Match.
NOT STEAM TECHNOLOGY.
GWEN, WATCH OUT BELOW YOU!
TAKE THAT! AND THAT!
AND--WHOOPS!!

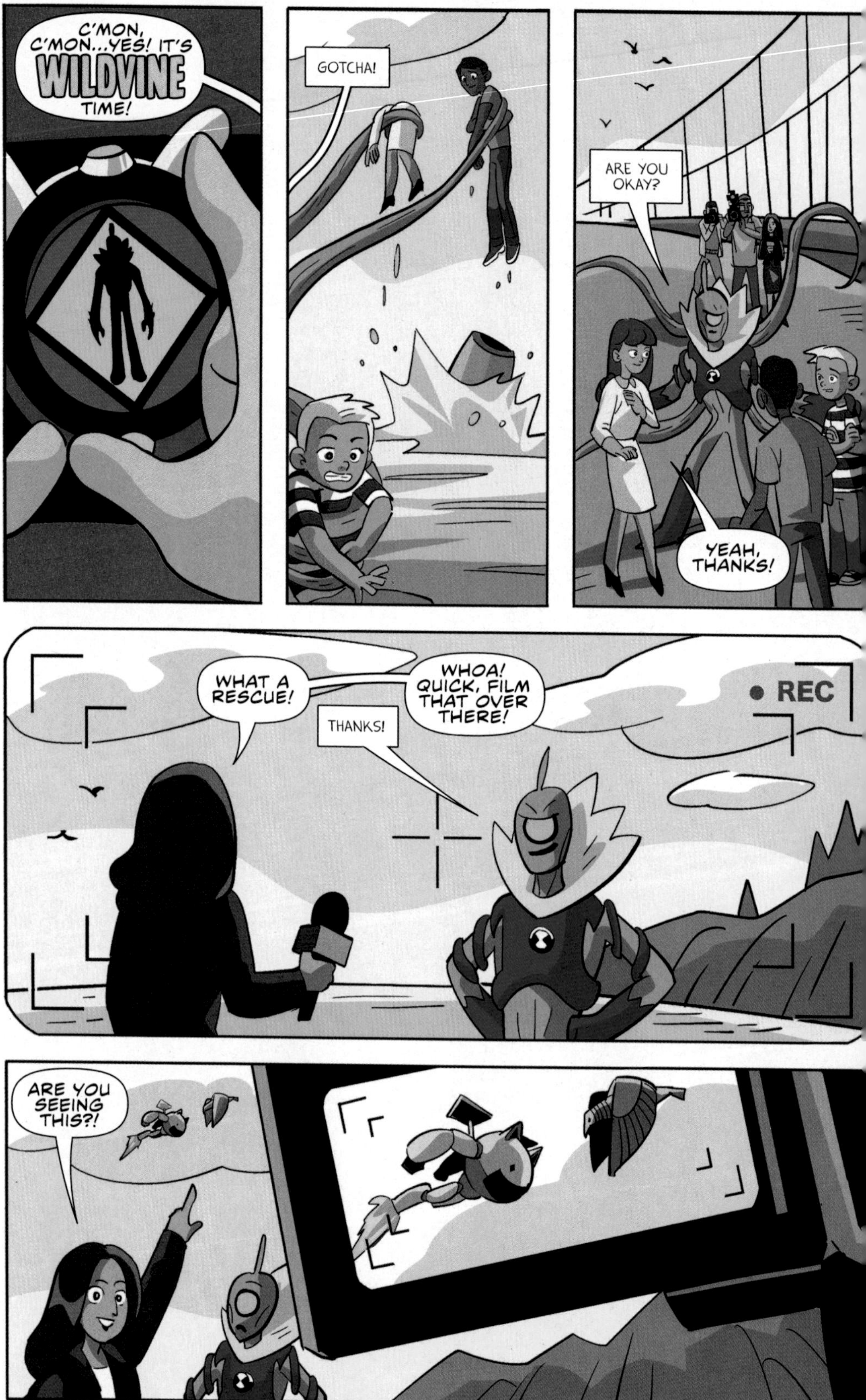
C'MON, C'MON...YES! IT'S WILDVINE TIME!
GOTCHA!
ARE YOU OKAY?
YEAH, THANKS!
WHAT A RESCUE!
WHOA! QUICK, FILM THAT OVER THERE!
THANKS!
REC
ARE YOU SEEING THIS?!

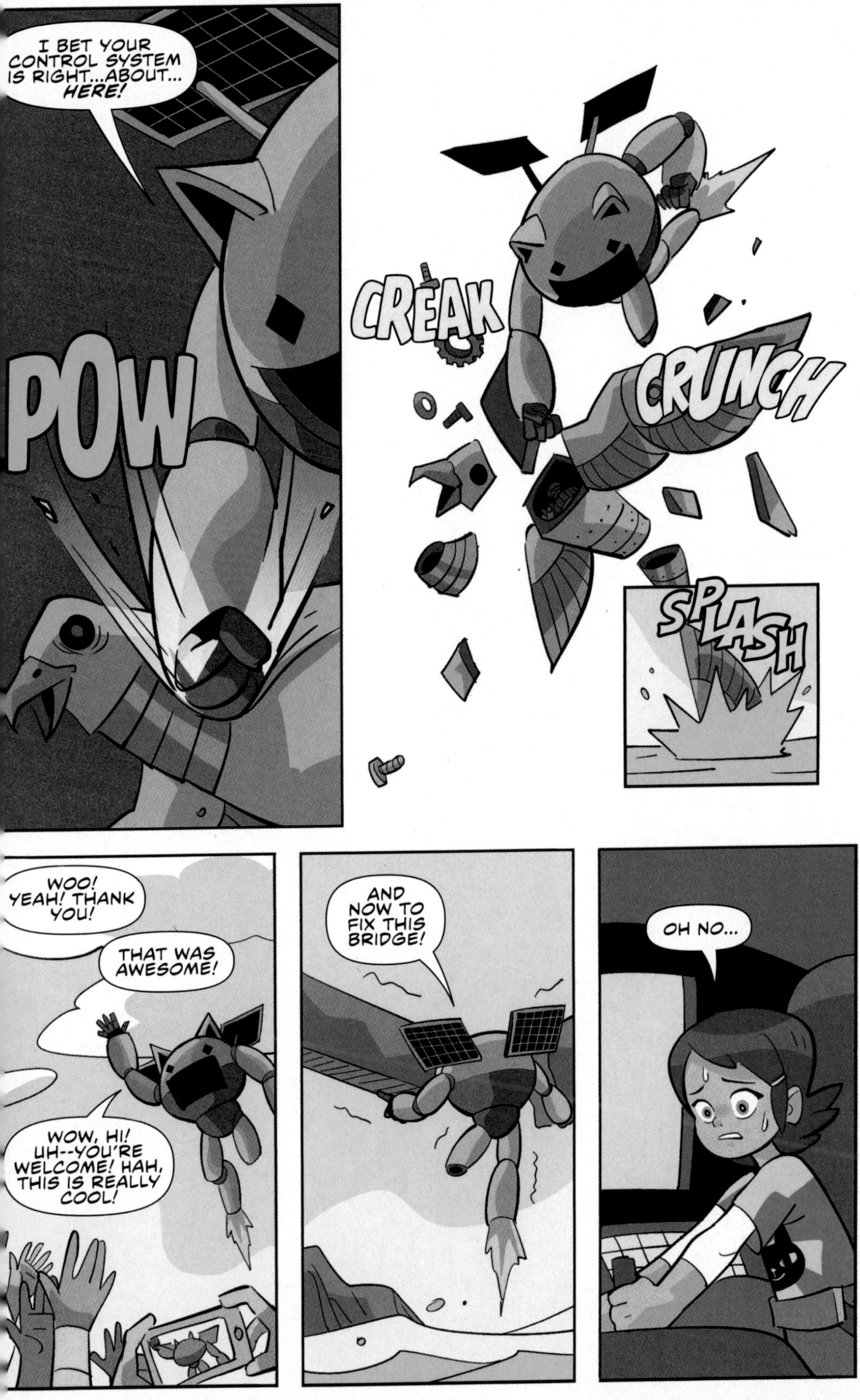
I BET YOUR CONTROL SYSTEM IS RIGHT...ABOUT... HERE!
POW
CREAK
CRUNCH
SPLASH
WOO! YEAH! THANK YOU!
THAT WAS AWESOME!
WOW, HI! UH--YOU'RE WELCOME! HAH, THIS IS REALLY COOL!
AND NOW TO FIX THIS BRIDGE!
OH NO...

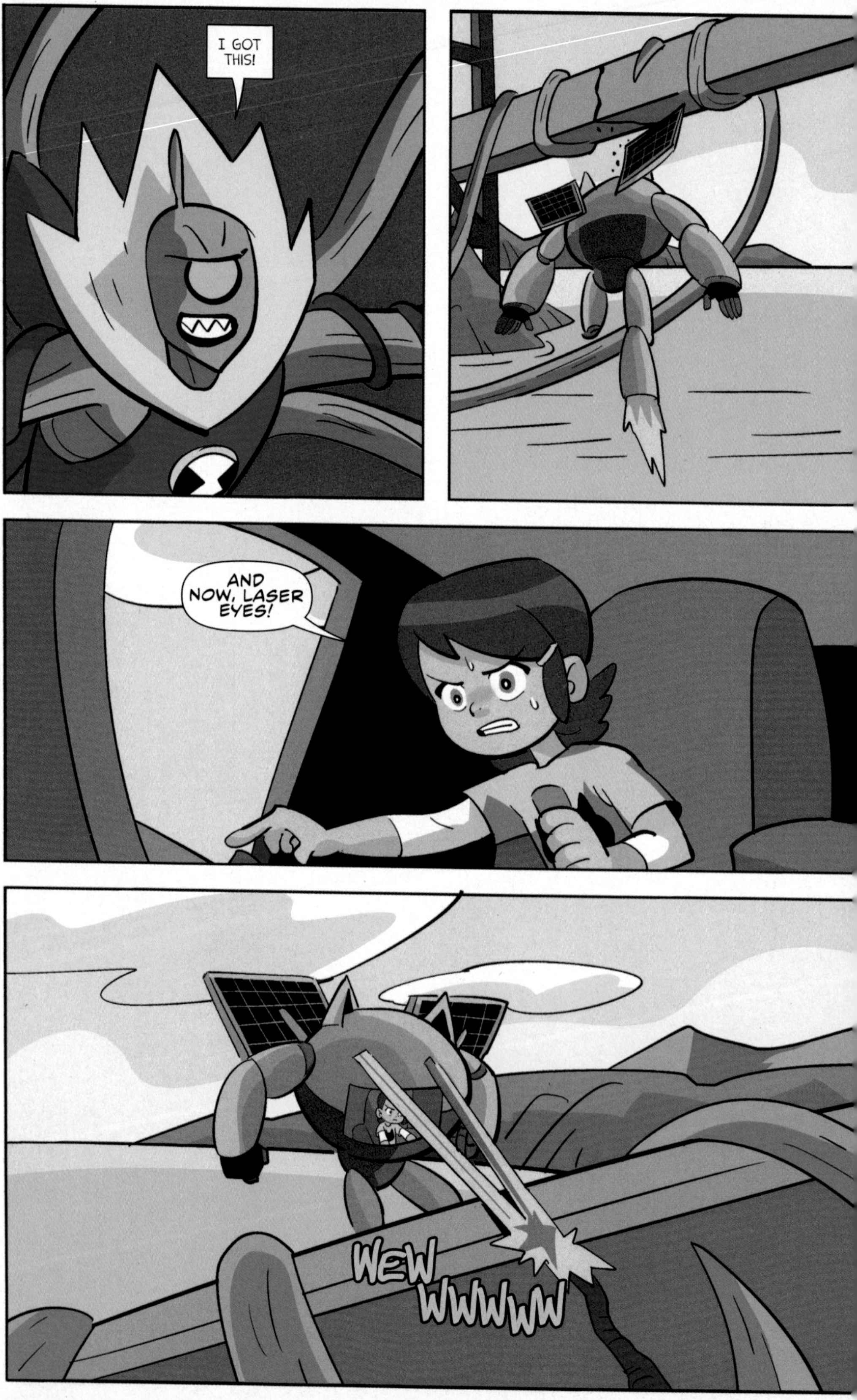
I GOT THIS!
AND NOW, LASER EYES!
WEW WWWWW

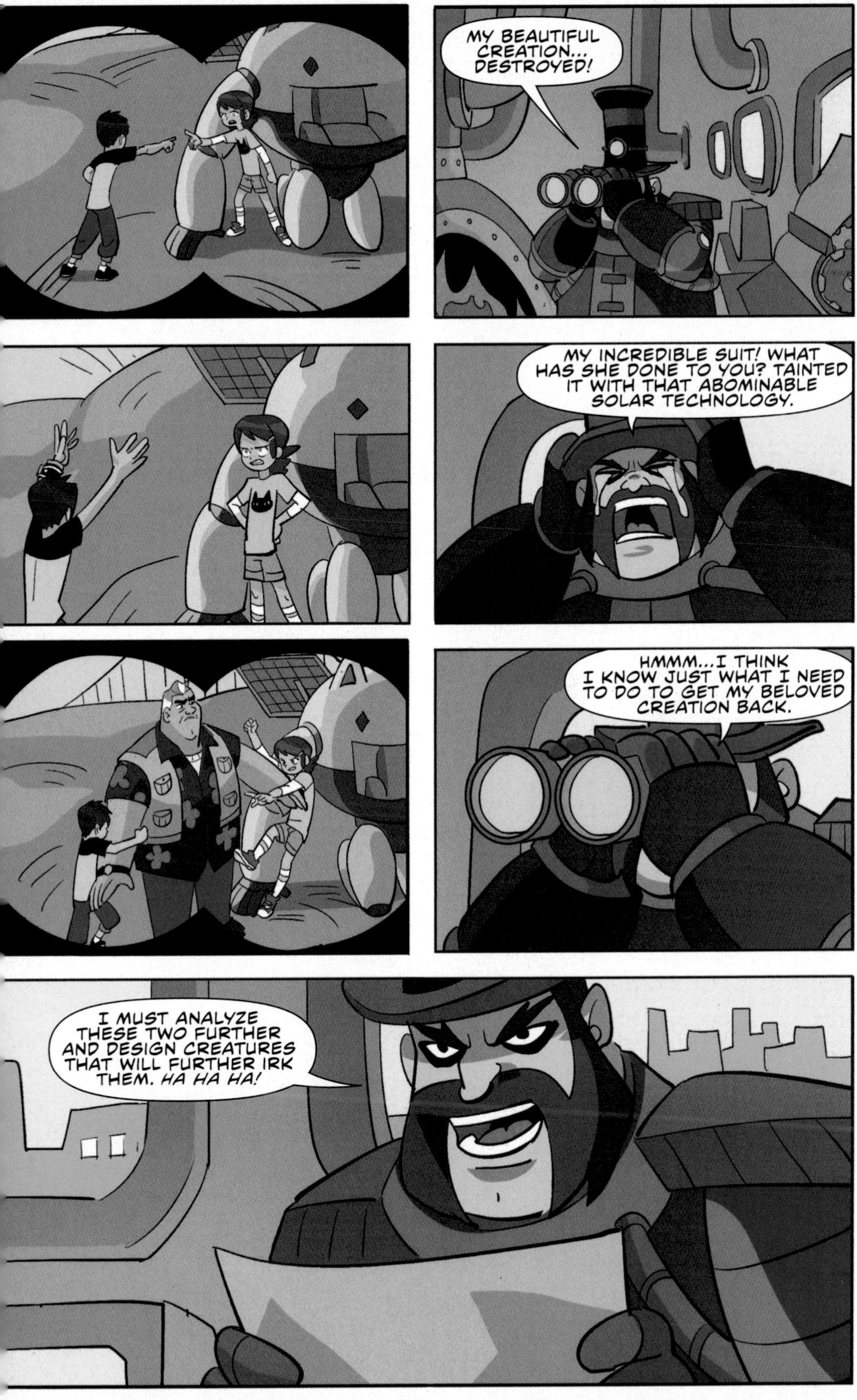

MY BEAUTIFUL CREATION... DESTROYED!
MY INCREDIBLE SUIT! WHAT HAS SHE DONE TO YOU? TAINTED IT WITH THAT ABOMINABLE SOLAR TECHNOLOGY.
HMMM...I THINK I KNOW JUST WHAT I NEED TO DO TO GET MY BELOVED CREATION BACK.
I MUST ANALYZE THESE TWO FURTHER AND DESIGN CREATURES THAT WILL FURTHER IRK THEM. *HA HA HA!*

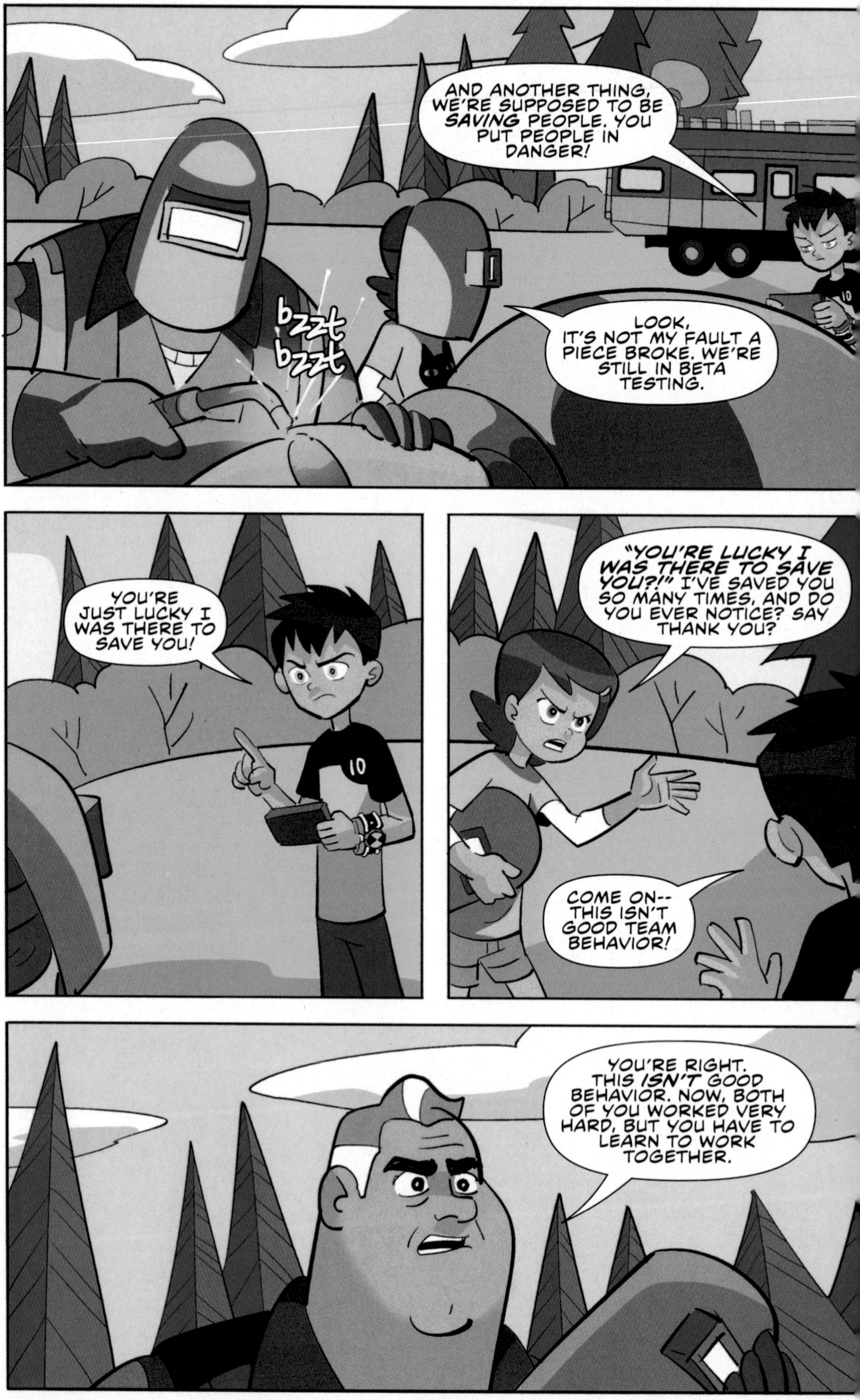
AND ANOTHER THING, WE'RE SUPPOSED TO BE SAVING PEOPLE. YOU PUT PEOPLE IN DANGER!
bzzt bzzt
LOOK, IT'S NOT MY FAULT A PIECE BROKE. WE'RE STILL IN BETA TESTING.
YOU'RE JUST LUCKY I WAS THERE TO SAVE YOU!
"YOU'RE LUCKY I WAS THERE TO SAVE YOU?!" I'VE SAVED YOU SO MANY TIMES, AND DO YOU EVER NOTICE? SAY THANK YOU?
COME ON-- THIS ISN'T GOOD TEAM BEHAVIOR!
YOU'RE RIGHT. THIS ISN'T GOOD BEHAVIOR. NOW, BOTH OF YOU WORKED VERY HARD, BUT YOU HAVE TO LEARN TO WORK TOGETHER.

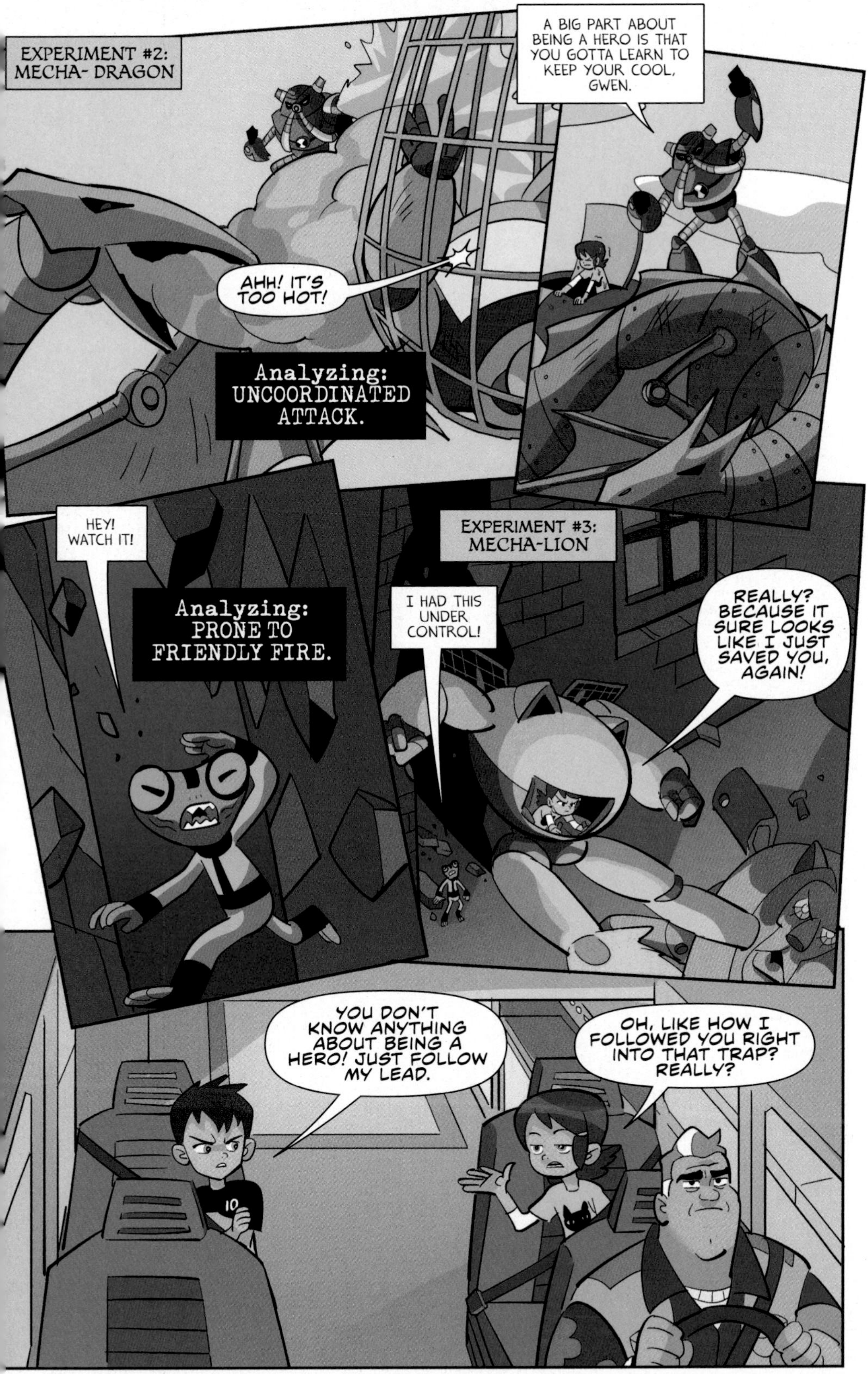
EXPERIMENT #2: MECHA- DRAGON
AHH! IT'S TOO HOT!
Analyzing: UNCOORDINATED ATTACK.
A BIG PART ABOUT BEING A HERO IS THAT YOU GOTTA LEARN TO KEEP YOUR COOL, GWEN.
HEY! WATCH IT!
Analyzing: PRONE TO FRIENDLY FIRE.
EXPERIMENT #3: MECHA-LION
I HAD THIS UNDER CONTROL!
REALLY? BECAUSE IT SURE LOOKS LIKE I JUST SAVED YOU, AGAIN!
YOU DON'T KNOW ANYTHING ABOUT BEING A HERO! JUST FOLLOW MY LEAD.
OH, LIKE HOW I FOLLOWED YOU RIGHT INTO THAT TRAP? REALLY?

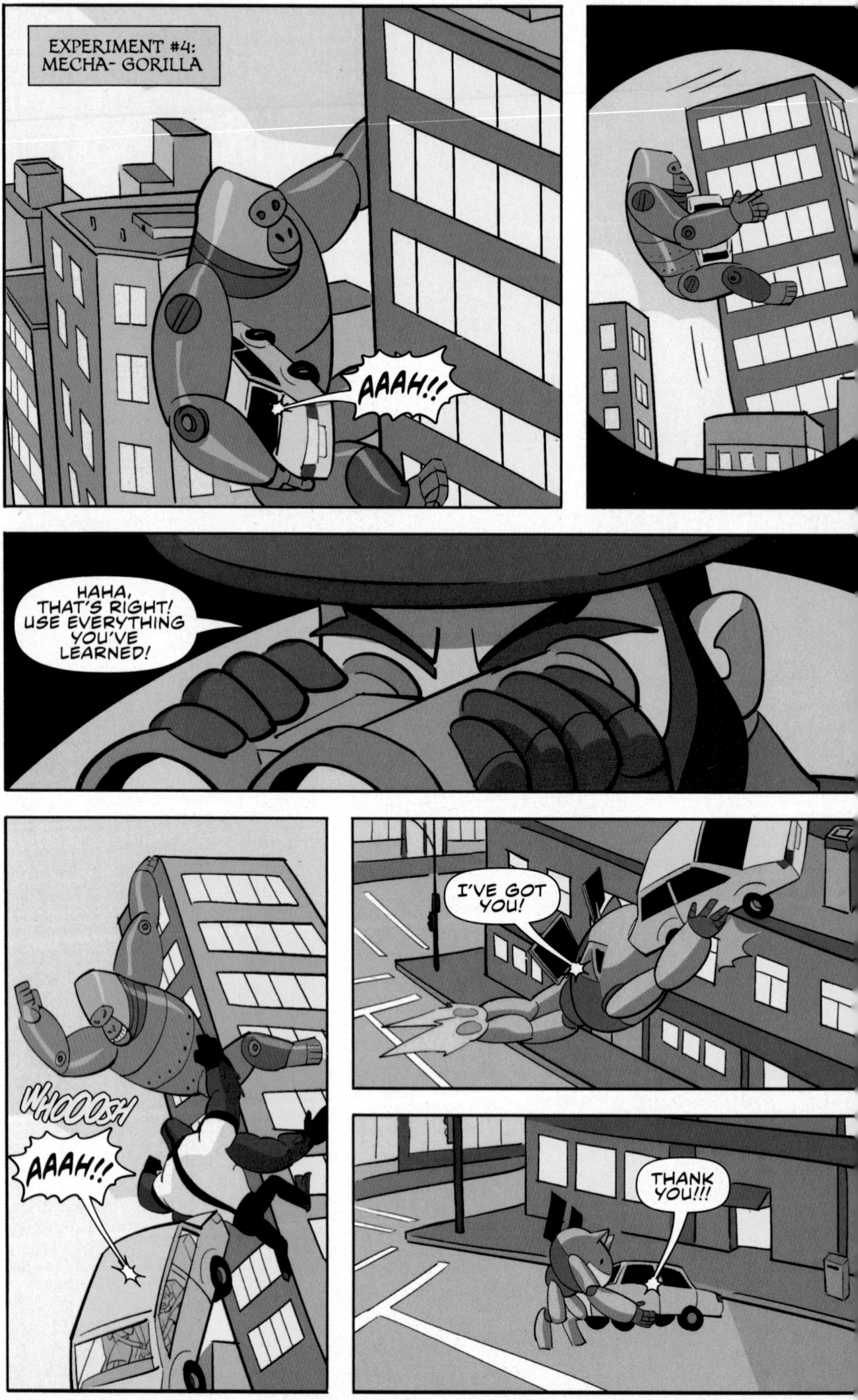
EXPERIMENT #4: MECHA- GORILLA
AAAH!!
HAHA, THAT'S RIGHT! USE EVERYTHING YOU'VE LEARNED!
WHOOOSH
AAAH!!
I'VE GOT YOU!
THANK YOU!!!

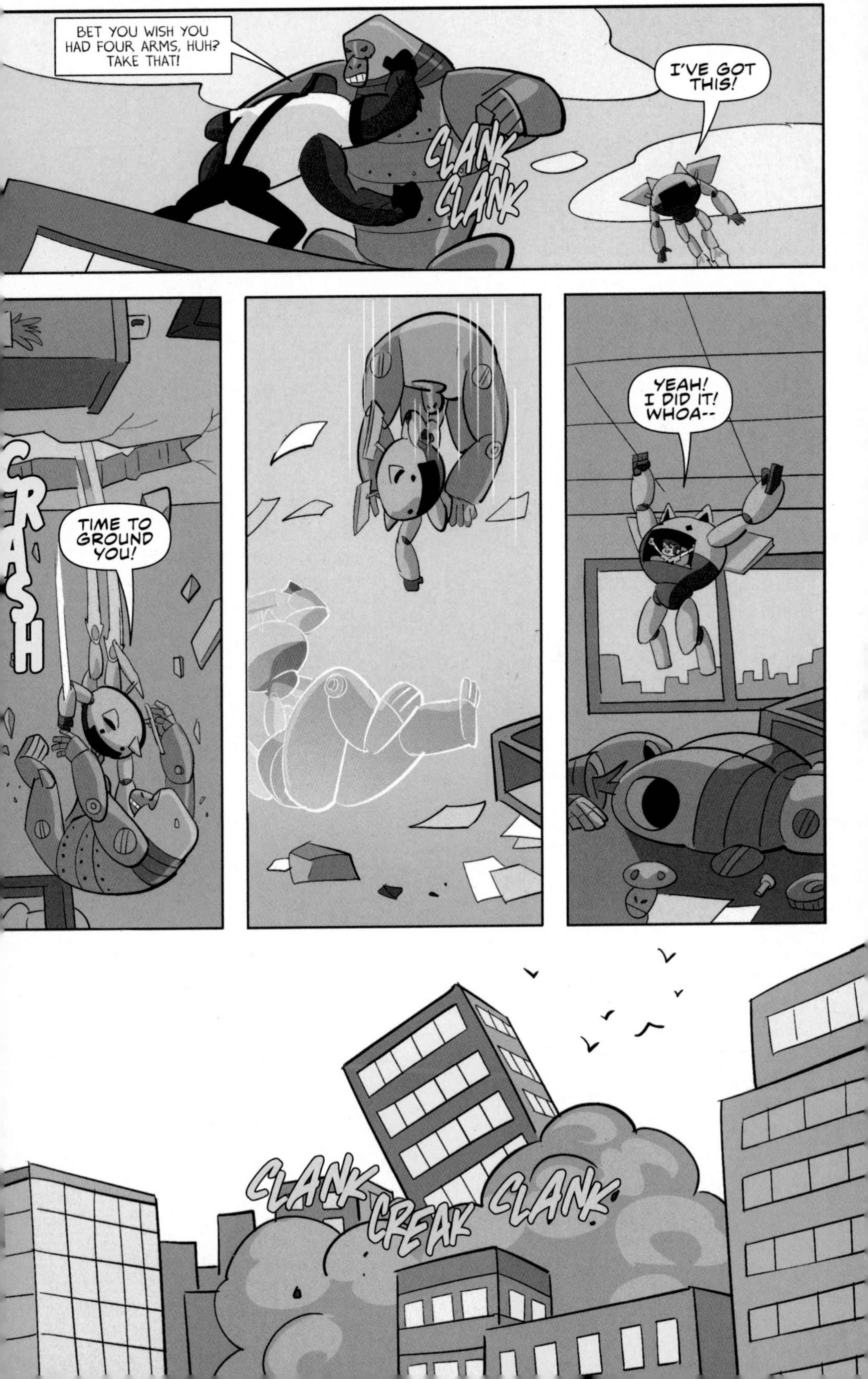
BET YOU WISH YOU HAD FOUR ARMS, HUH? TAKE THAT!
CLANK CLANK
I'VE GOT THIS!
CRASH
TIME TO GROUND YOU!
YEAH! I DID IT! WHOA--
CLANK CREAK CLANK

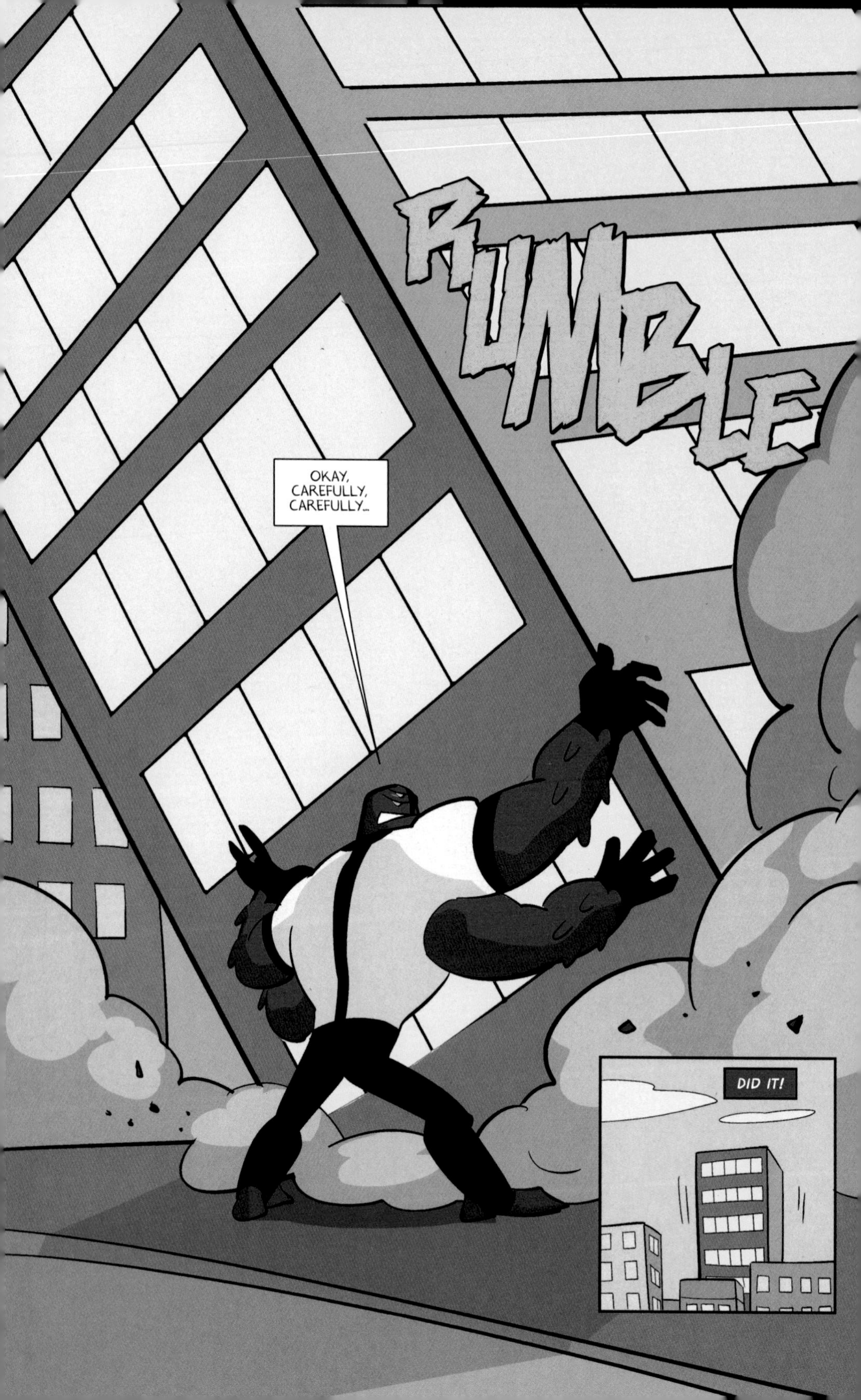
RUMBLE
OKAY, CAREFULLY, CAREFULLY...
DID IT!

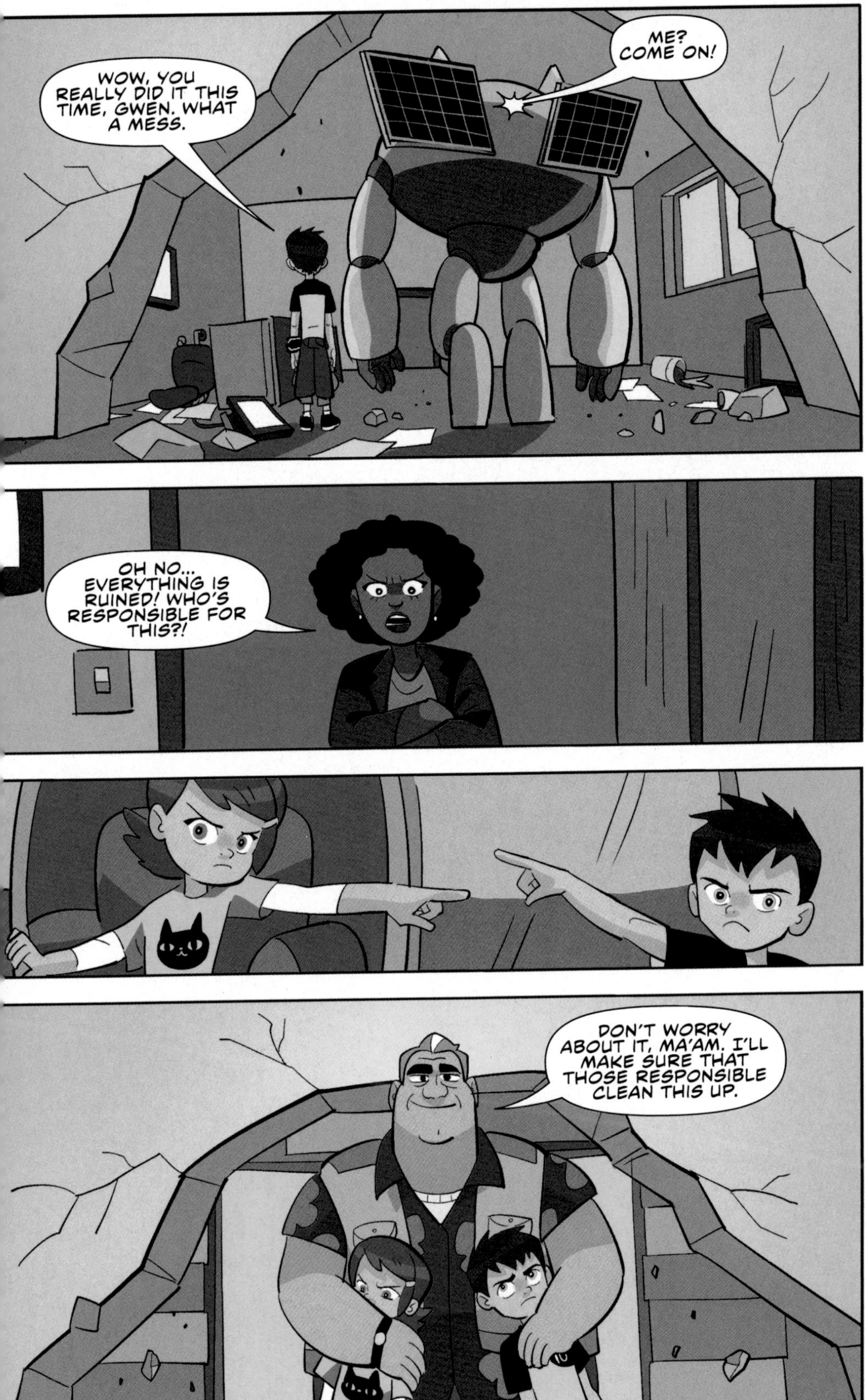
WOW, YOU REALLY DID IT THIS TIME, GWEN. WHAT A MESS.
ME? COME ON!
OH NO... EVERYTHING IS RUINED! WHO'S RESPONSIBLE FOR THIS?!
DON'T WORRY ABOUT IT, MA'AM. I'LL MAKE SURE THAT THOSE RESPONSIBLE CLEAN THIS UP.

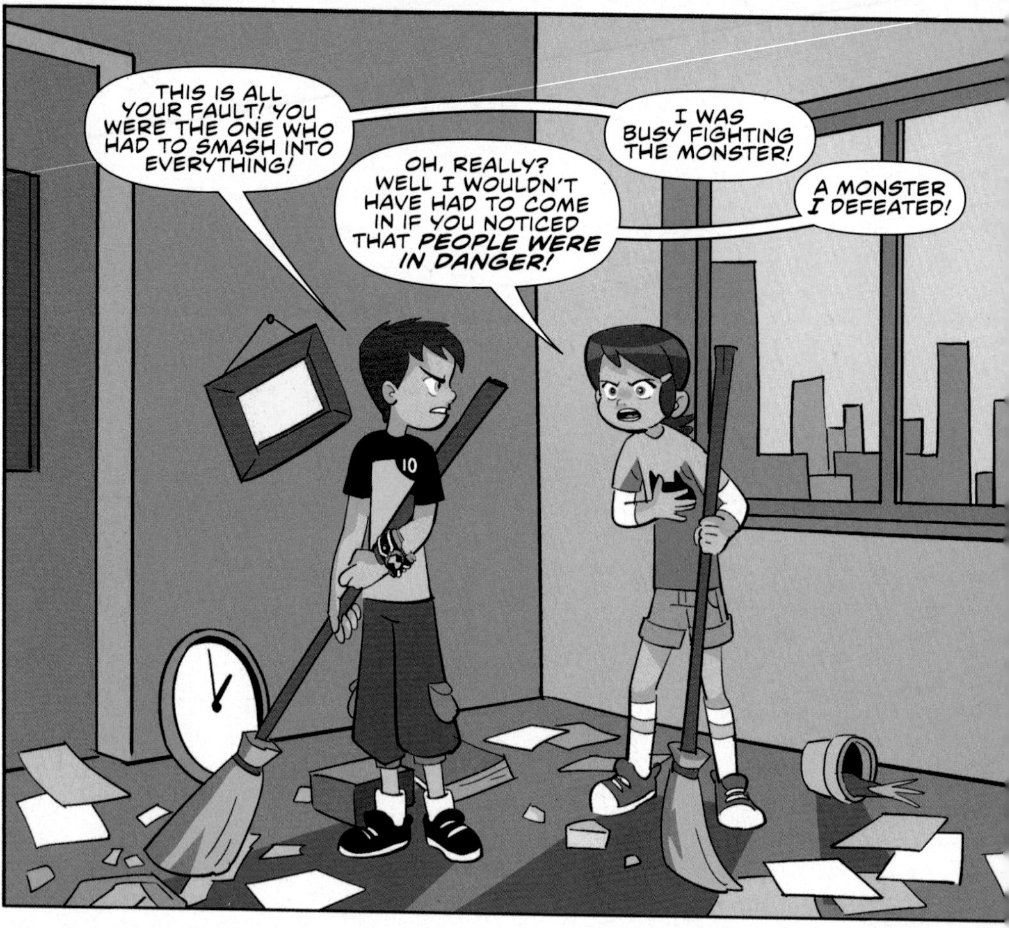
THIS IS ALL YOUR FAULT! YOU WERE THE ONE WHO HAD TO SMASH INTO EVERYTHING!
I WAS BUSY FIGHTING THE MONSTER!
OH, REALLY? WELL I WOULDN'T HAVE HAD TO COME IN IF YOU NOTICED THAT *PEOPLE WERE IN DANGER!*
A MONSTER *I* DEFEATED!

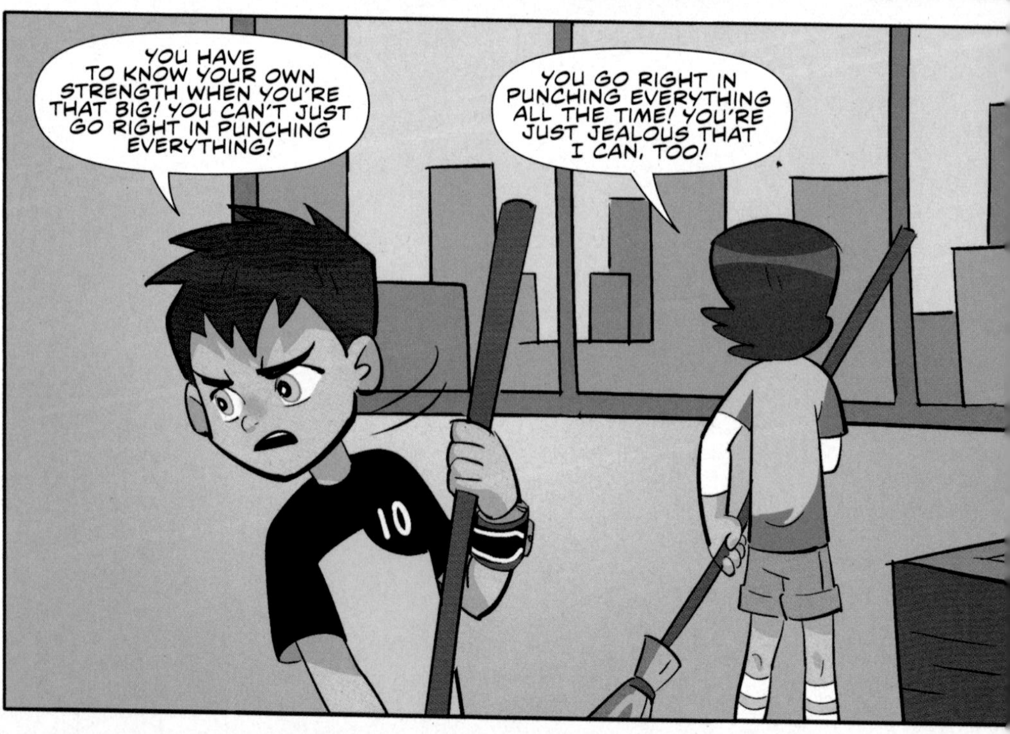
YOU HAVE TO KNOW YOUR OWN STRENGTH WHEN YOU'RE THAT BIG! YOU CAN'T JUST GO RIGHT IN PUNCHING EVERYTHING!
YOU GO RIGHT IN PUNCHING EVERYTHING ALL THE TIME! YOU'RE JUST JEALOUS THAT I CAN, TOO!

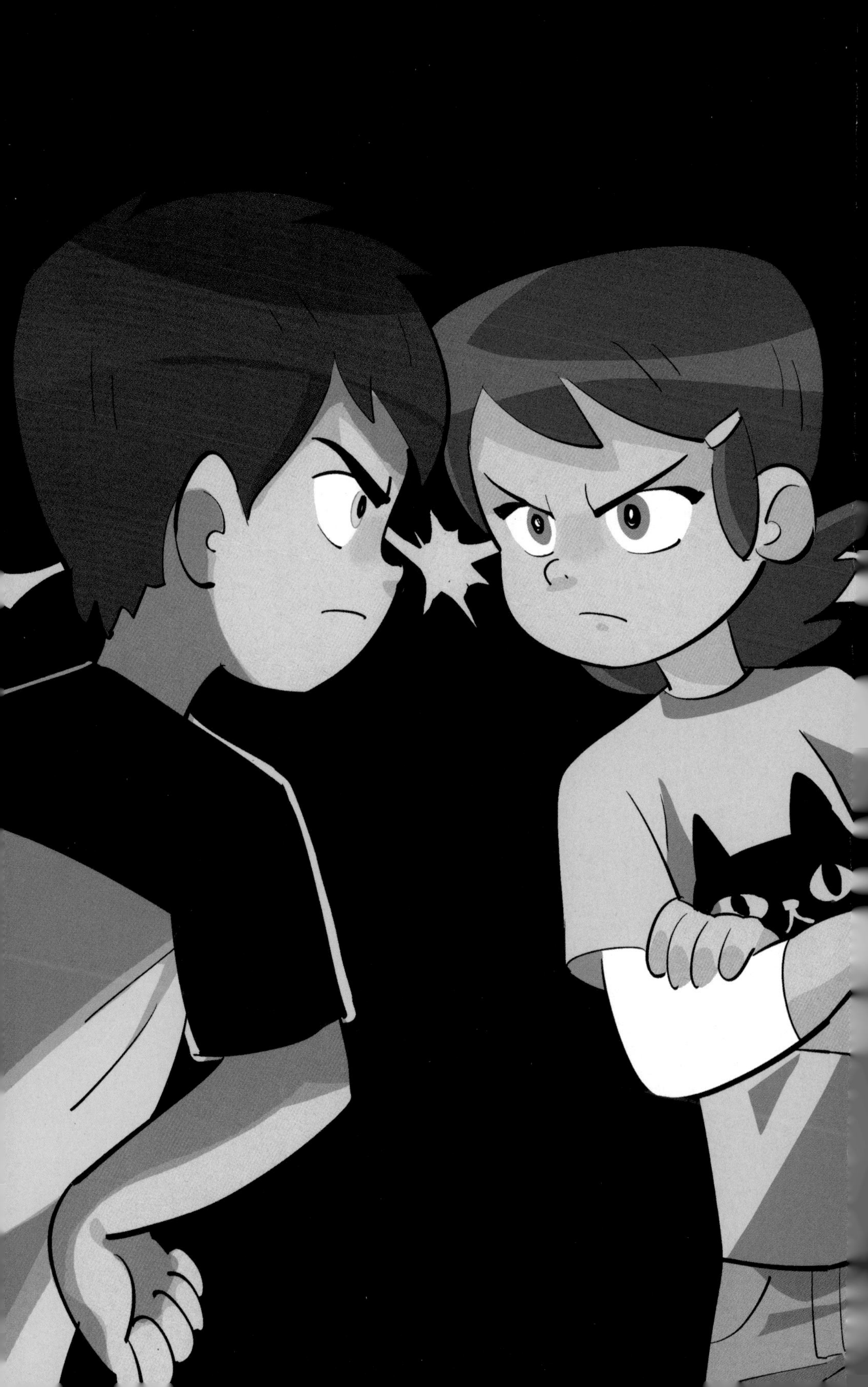

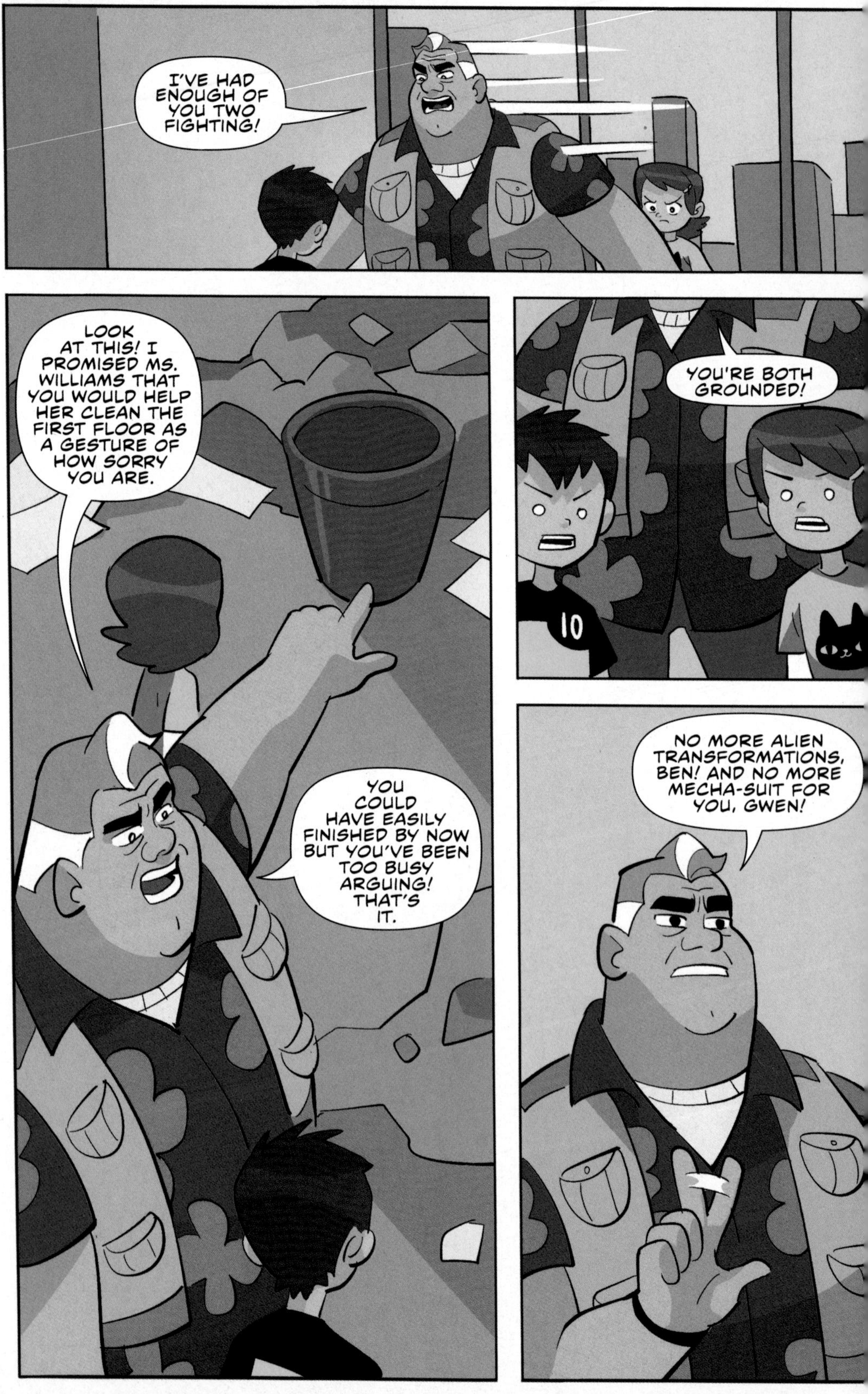
I'VE HAD ENOUGH OF YOU TWO FIGHTING!
LOOK AT THIS! I PROMISED MS. WILLIAMS THAT YOU WOULD HELP HER CLEAN THE FIRST FLOOR AS A GESTURE OF HOW SORRY YOU ARE.
YOU COULD HAVE EASILY FINISHED BY NOW BUT YOU'VE BEEN TOO BUSY ARGUING! THAT'S IT.
YOU'RE BOTH GROUNDED!
10
NO MORE ALIEN TRANSFORMATIONS, BEN! AND NO MORE MECHA-SUIT FOR YOU, GWEN!

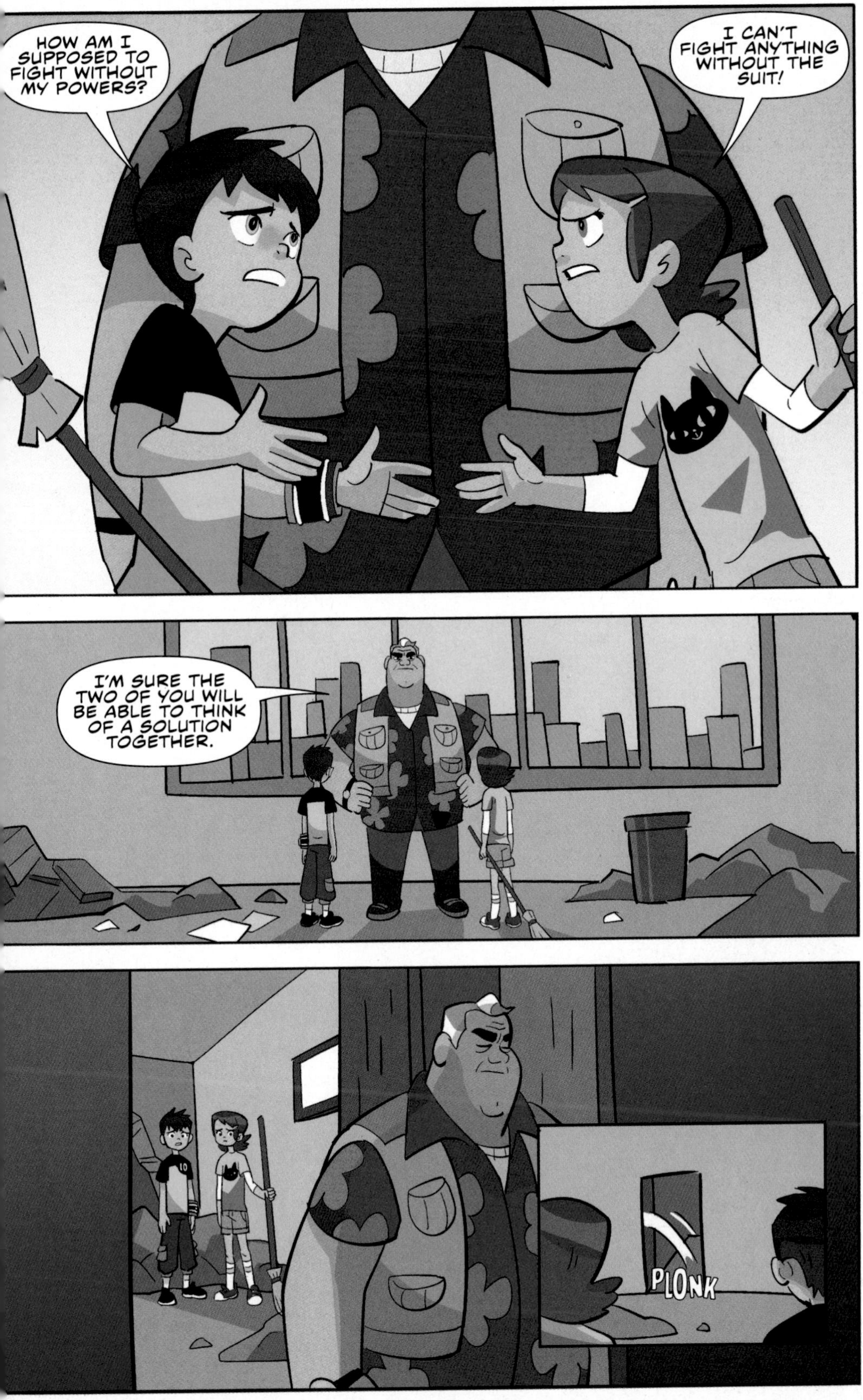
HOW AM I SUPPOSED TO FIGHT WITHOUT MY POWERS?
I CAN'T FIGHT ANYTHING WITHOUT THE SUIT!
I'M SURE THE TWO OF YOU WILL BE ABLE TO THINK OF A SOLUTION TOGETHER.
10
PLONK

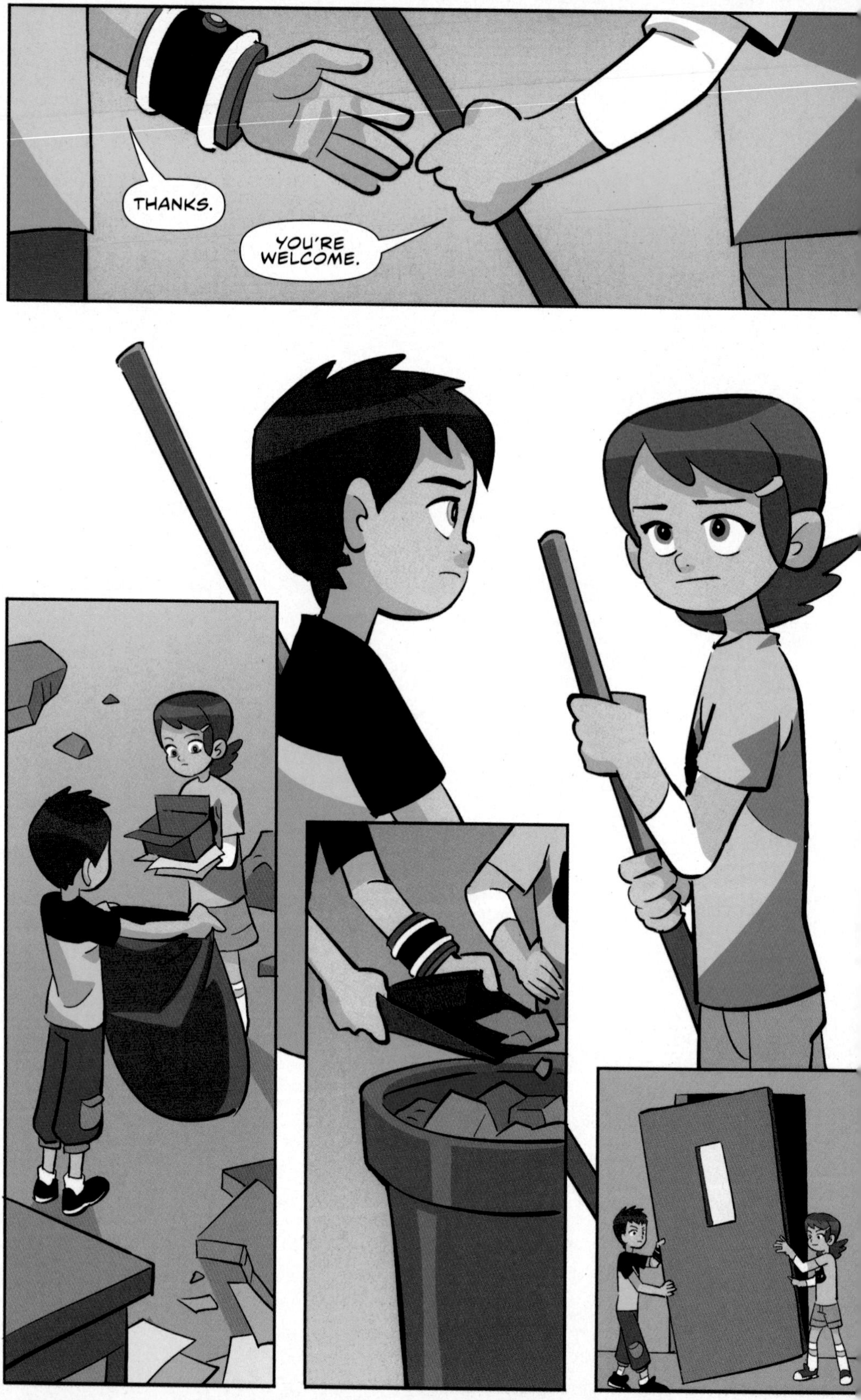
THANKS.
YOU'RE WELCOME.

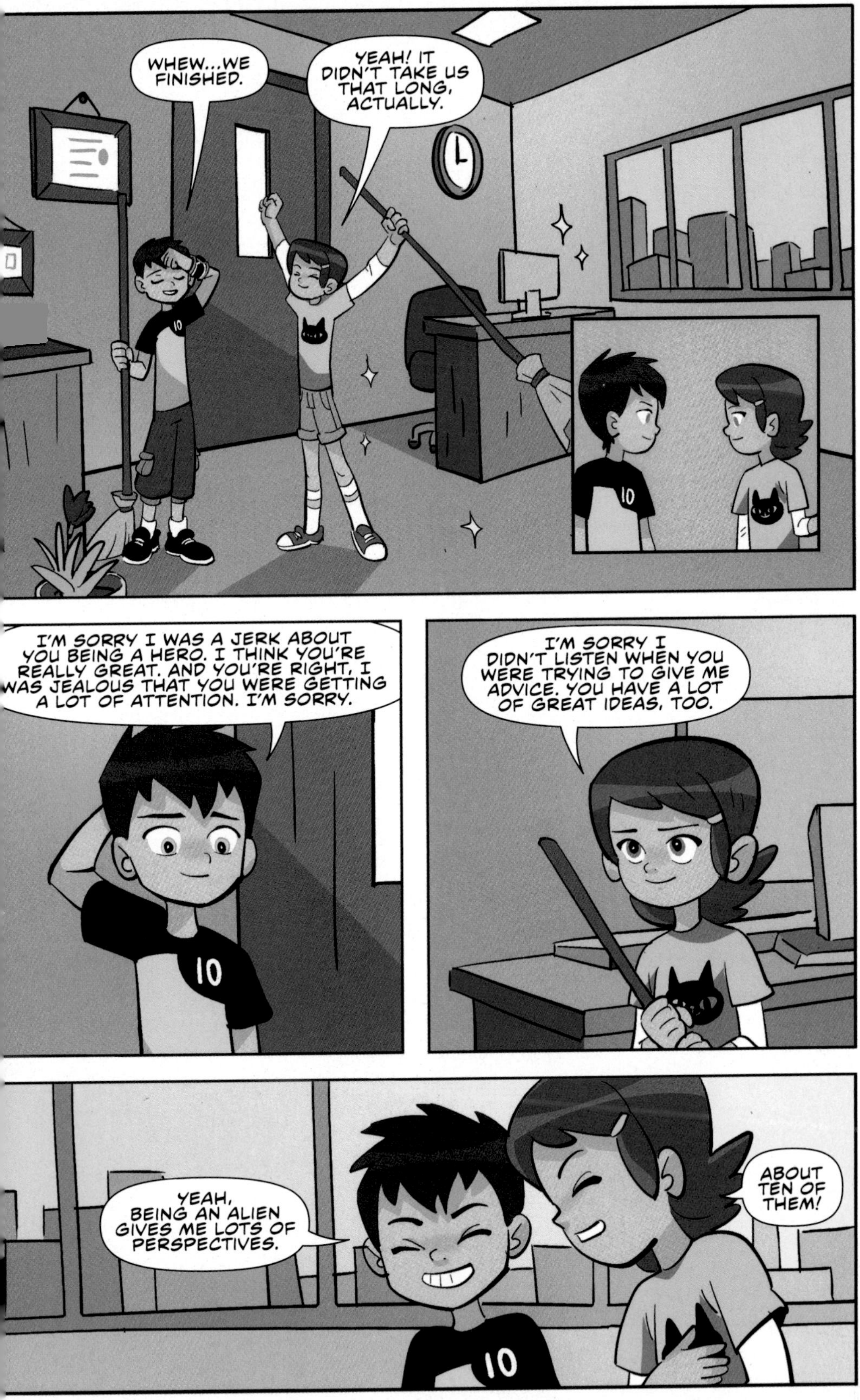
WHEW...WE FINISHED.
YEAH! IT DIDN'T TAKE US THAT LONG, ACTUALLY.
I'M SORRY I WAS A JERK ABOUT YOU BEING A HERO. I THINK YOU'RE REALLY GREAT. AND YOU'RE RIGHT, I WAS JEALOUS THAT YOU WERE GETTING A LOT OF ATTENTION. I'M SORRY.
I'M SORRY I DIDN'T LISTEN WHEN YOU WERE TRYING TO GIVE ME ADVICE. YOU HAVE A LOT OF GREAT IDEAS, TOO.
YEAH, BEING AN ALIEN GIVES ME LOTS OF PERSPECTIVES.
ABOUT TEN OF THEM!

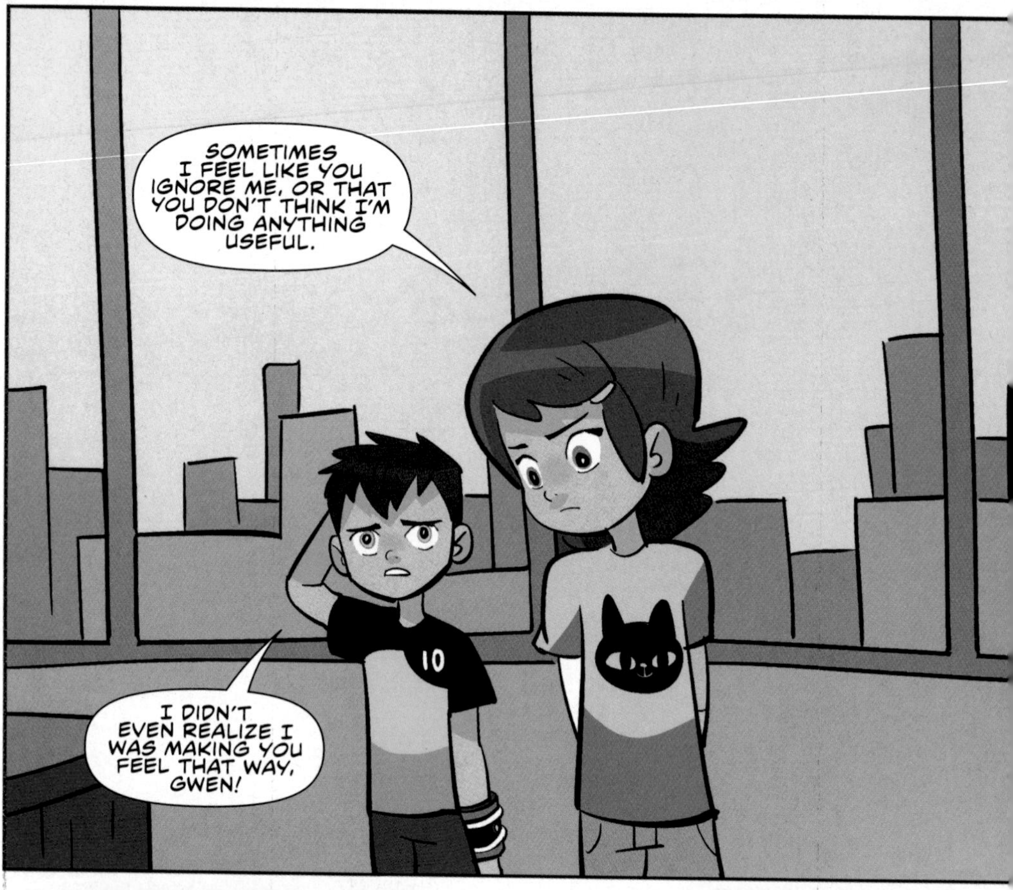
SOMETIMES I FEEL LIKE YOU IGNORE ME, OR THAT YOU DON'T THINK I'M DOING ANYTHING USEFUL.
I DIDN'T EVEN REALIZE I WAS MAKING YOU FEEL THAT WAY, GWEN!
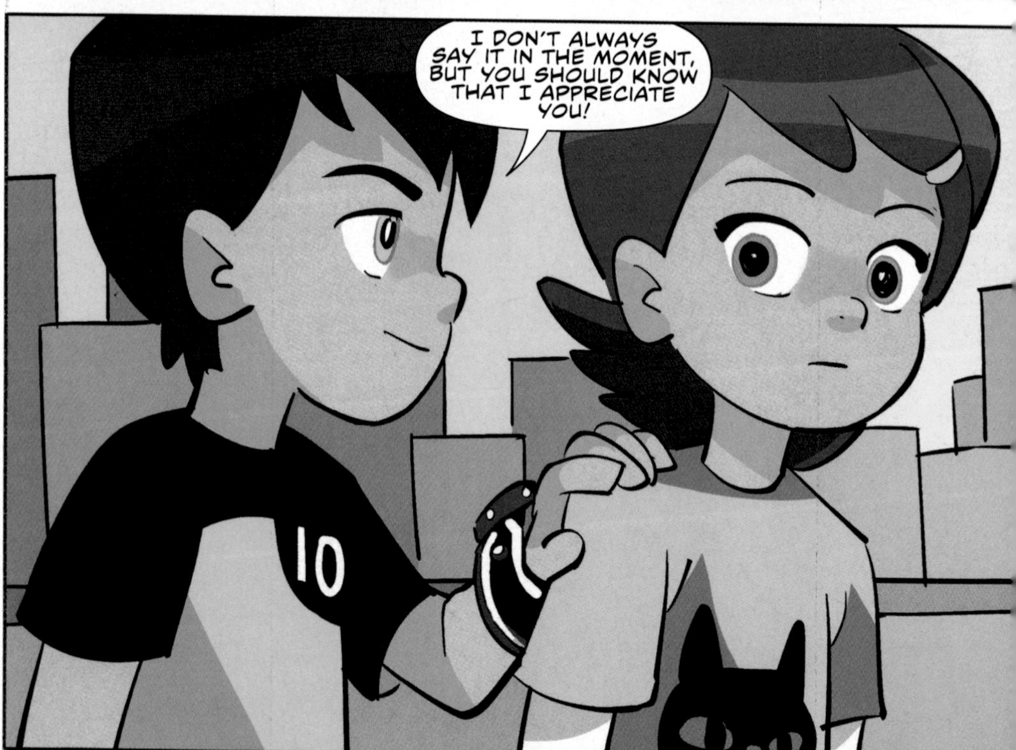
I DON'T ALWAYS SAY IT IN THE MOMENT, BUT YOU SHOULD KNOW THAT I APPRECIATE YOU!

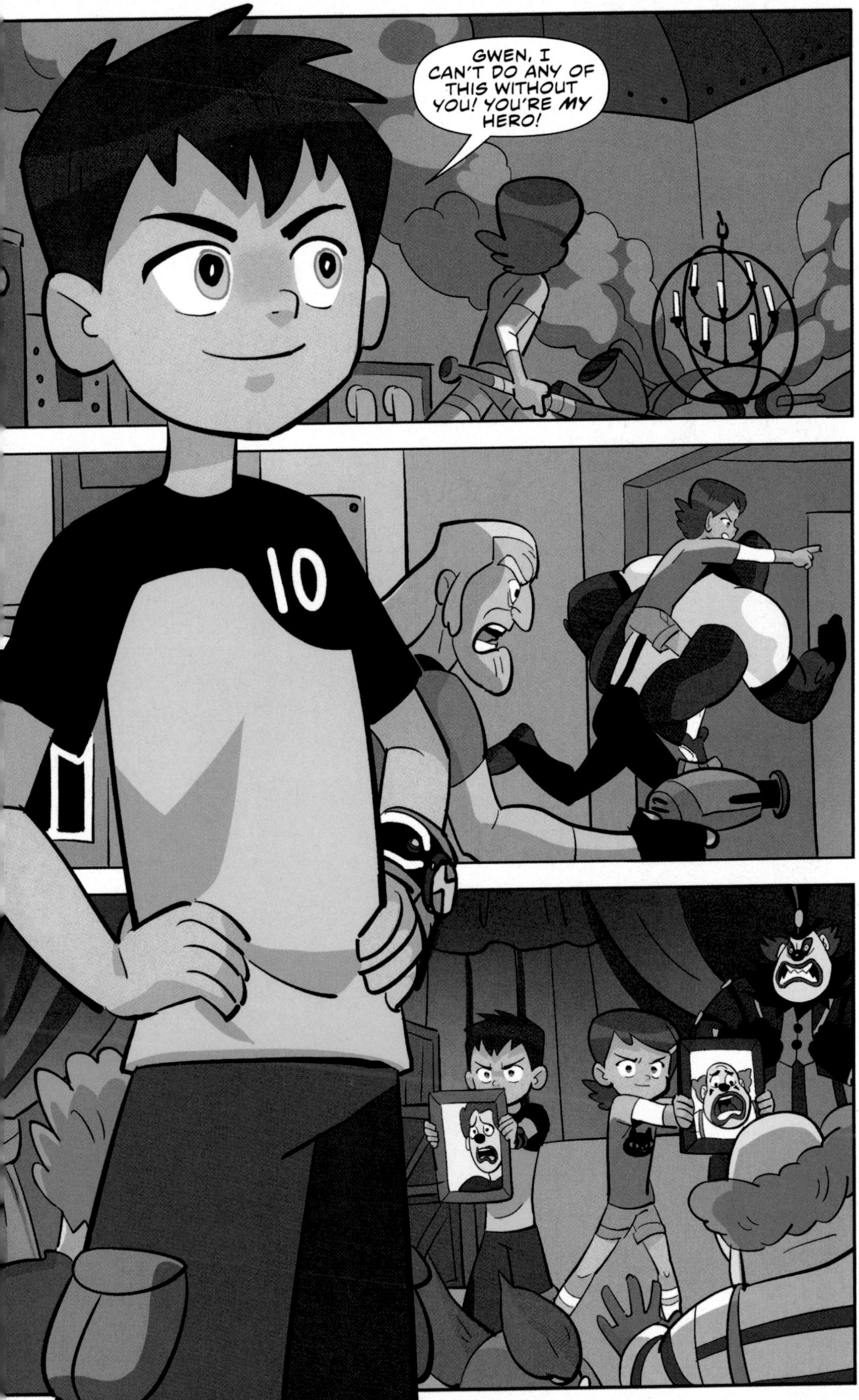
GWEN, I CAN'T DO ANY OF THIS WITHOUT YOU! YOU'RE MY HERO!
10

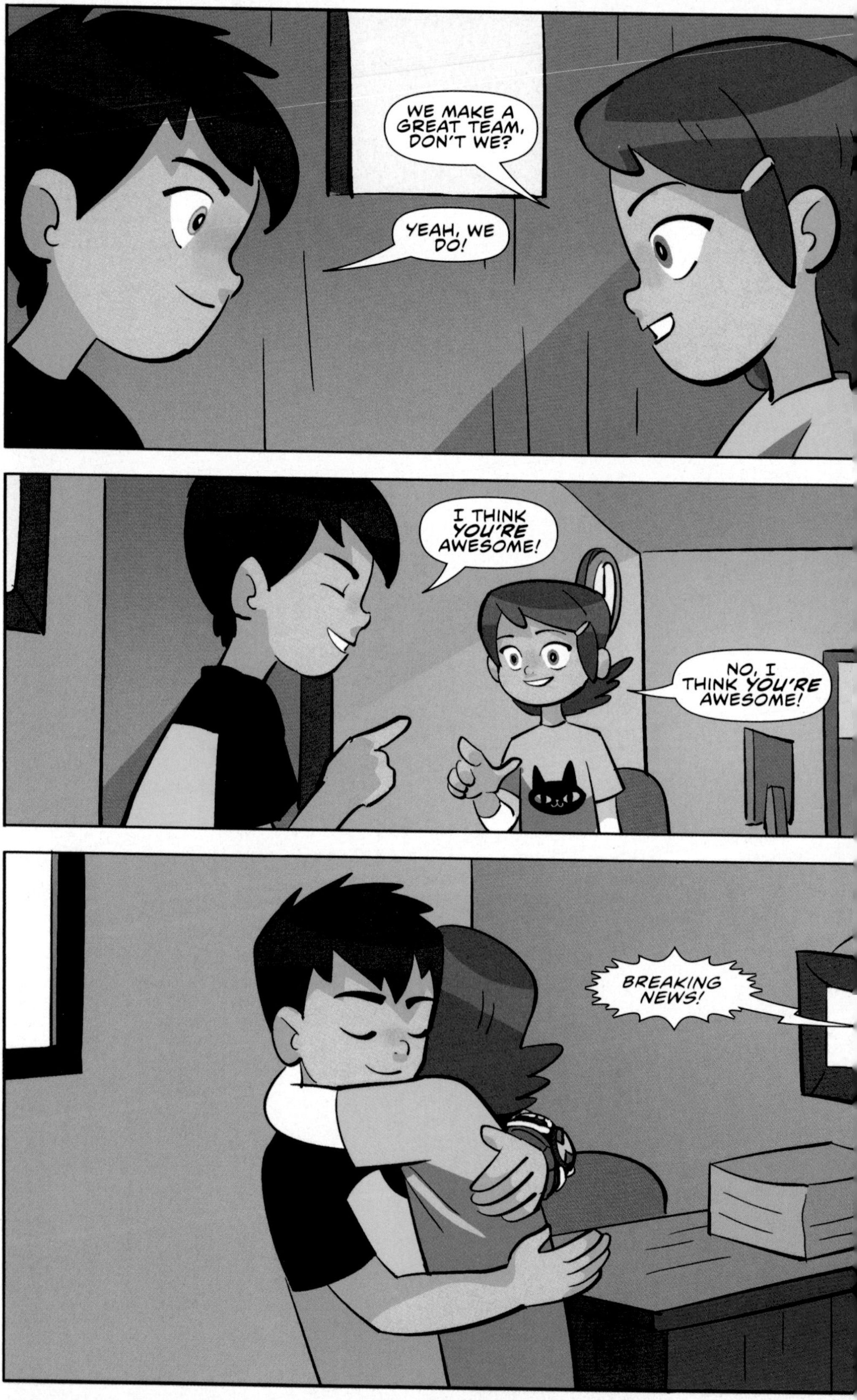
WE MAKE A GREAT TEAM, DON'T WE?
YEAH, WE DO!
I THINK YOU'RE AWESOME!
NO, I THINK YOU'RE AWESOME!
BREAKING NEWS!

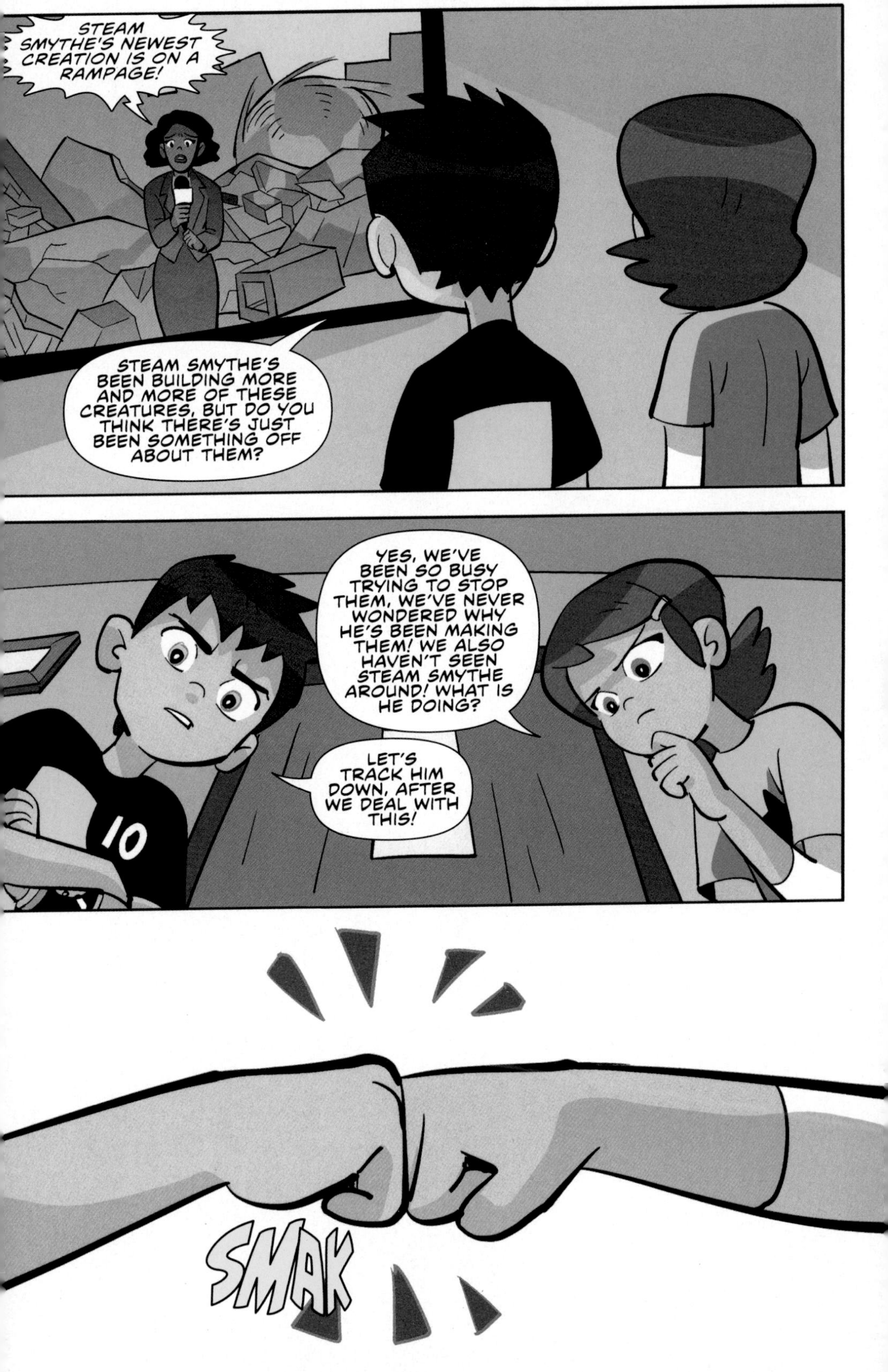
STEAM SMYTHE'S NEWEST CREATION IS ON A RAMPAGE!
STEAM SMYTHE'S BEEN BUILDING MORE AND MORE OF THESE CREATURES, BUT DO YOU THINK THERE'S JUST BEEN SOMETHING OFF ABOUT THEM?
YES, WE'VE BEEN SO BUSY TRYING TO STOP THEM, WE'VE NEVER WONDERED WHY HE'S BEEN MAKING THEM! WE ALSO HAVEN'T SEEN STEAM SMYTHE AROUND! WHAT IS HE DOING?
LET'S TRACK HIM DOWN, AFTER WE DEAL WITH THIS!
10
SMAK

HA HA HA! WHILE ALL THE AUTHORITIES ARE BEING DISTRACTED BY MY MECHA-DILLOW, I'M GETTING AWAY WITH THE BIGGEST HEISTS OF THE CENTURY.

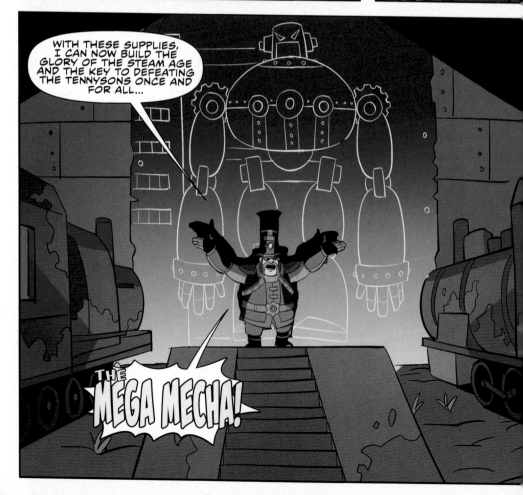

WITH THESE SUPPLIES, I CAN NOW BUILD THE GLORY OF THE STEAM AGE AND THE KEY TO DEFEATING THE TENNYSONS ONCE AND FOR ALL...

THE MEGA MECHA!

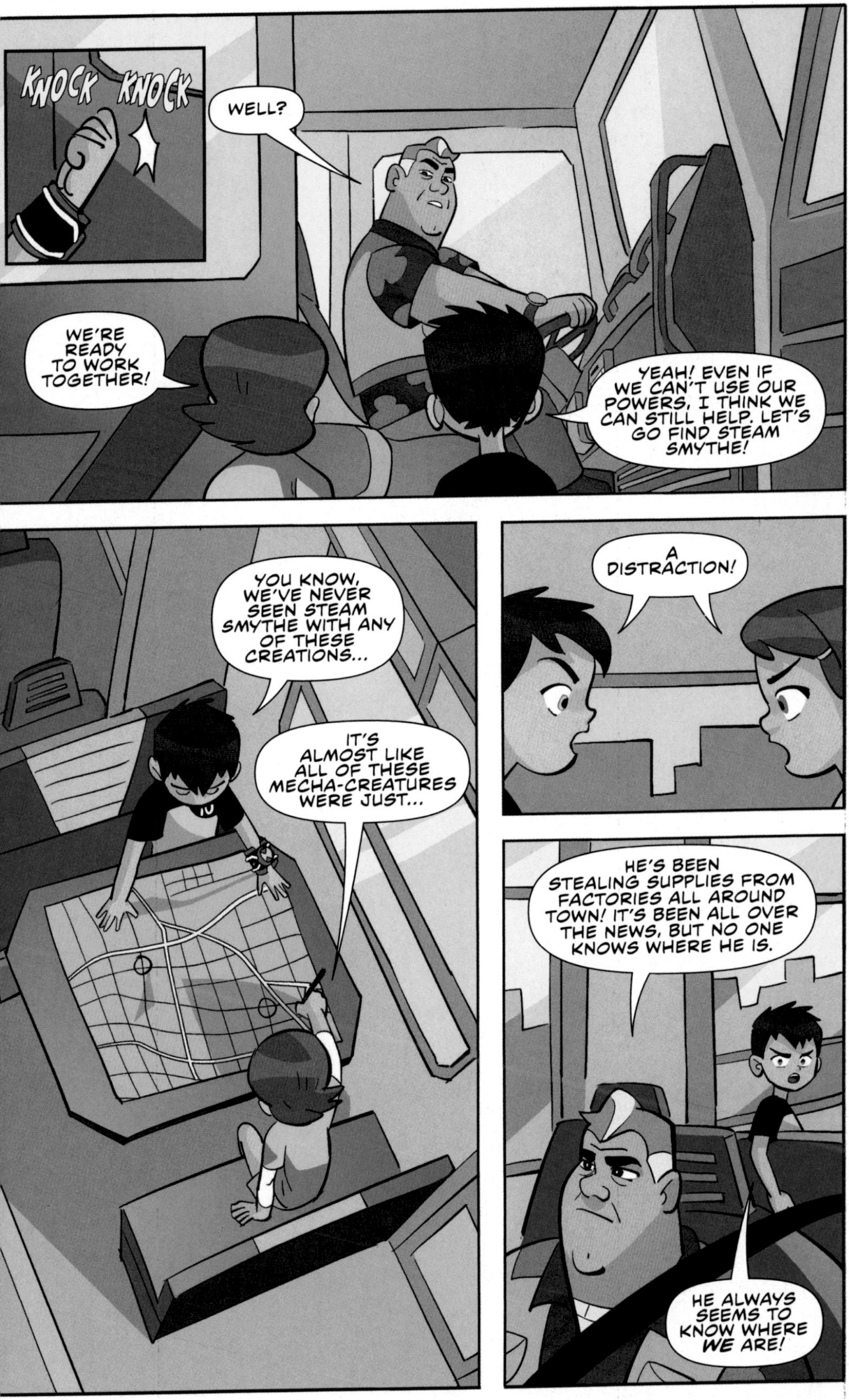
KNOCK KNOCK
WELL?
WE'RE READY TO WORK TOGETHER!
YEAH! EVEN IF WE CAN'T USE OUR POWERS, I THINK WE CAN STILL HELP. LET'S GO FIND STEAM SMYTHE!
YOU KNOW, WE'VE NEVER SEEN STEAM SMYTHE WITH ANY OF THESE CREATIONS...
IT'S ALMOST LIKE ALL OF THESE MECHA-CREATURES WERE JUST...
A DISTRACTION!
HE'S BEEN STEALING SUPPLIES FROM FACTORIES ALL AROUND TOWN! IT'S BEEN ALL OVER THE NEWS, BUT NO ONE KNOWS WHERE HE IS.
HE ALWAYS SEEMS TO KNOW WHERE WE ARE!

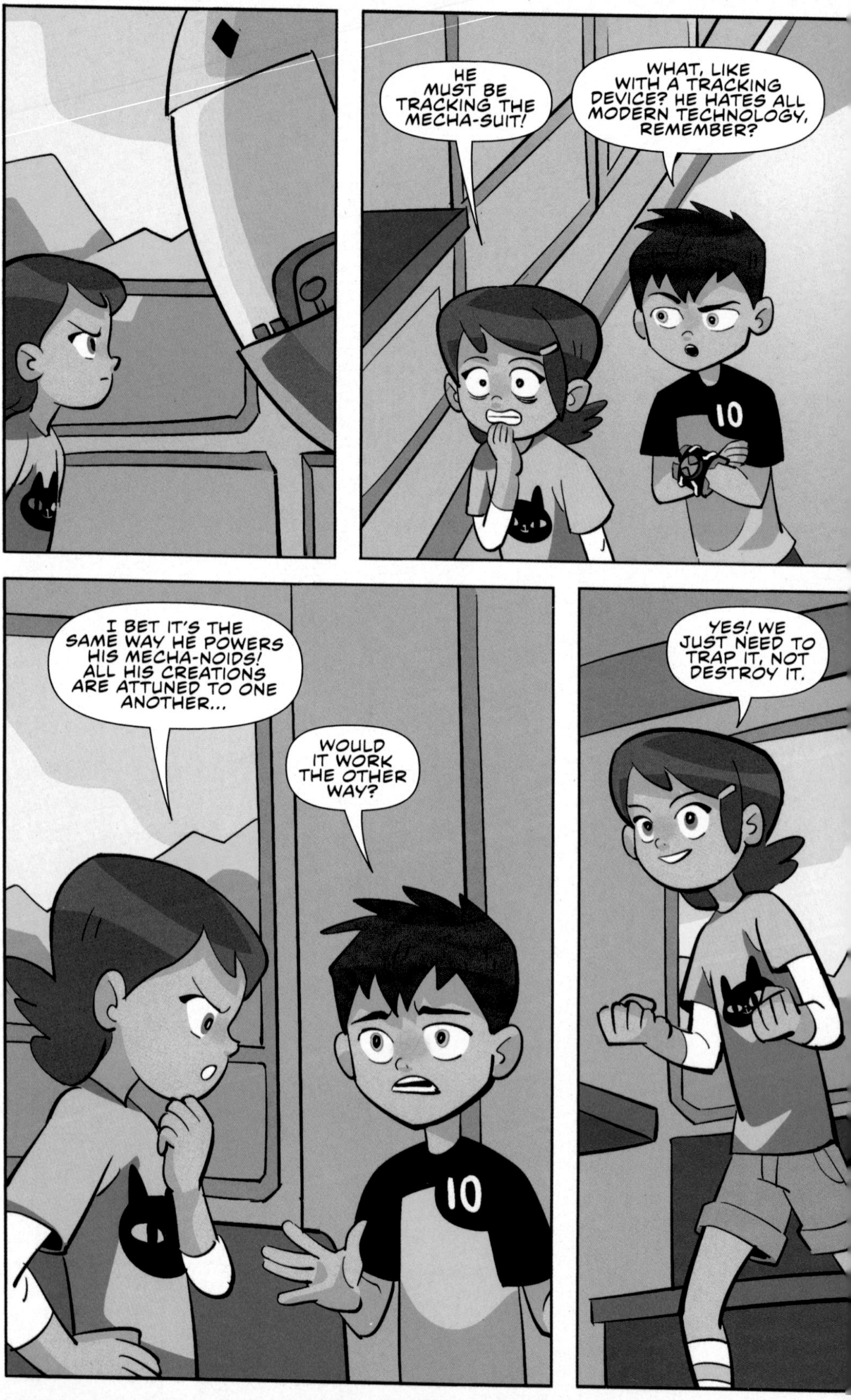
HE MUST BE TRACKING THE MECHA-SUIT!
WHAT, LIKE WITH A TRACKING DEVICE? HE HATES ALL MODERN TECHNOLOGY, REMEMBER?
10
I BET IT'S THE SAME WAY HE POWERS HIS MECHA-NOIDS! ALL HIS CREATIONS ARE ATTUNED TO ONE ANOTHER...
WOULD IT WORK THE OTHER WAY?
YES! WE JUST NEED TO TRAP IT, NOT DESTROY IT.
10

THIS JUST IN, THE GIANT ROBOTIC ARMADILLO IS ROLLING THROUGH DOWNTOWN AND HEADING SOUTH!

SOUNDS LIKE A SOLID PLAN, BUT YOU'RE GONNA HAVE TO MOVE! THIS THING SOUNDS FAST!

ALRIGHT, FIRST WE HAVE TO STOP IT. ANY IDEAS?

HMM...

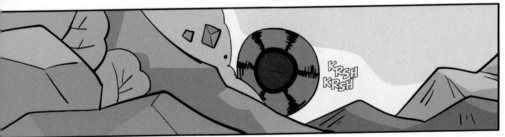

KRSH KRSH

I DON'T THINK WE CAN!

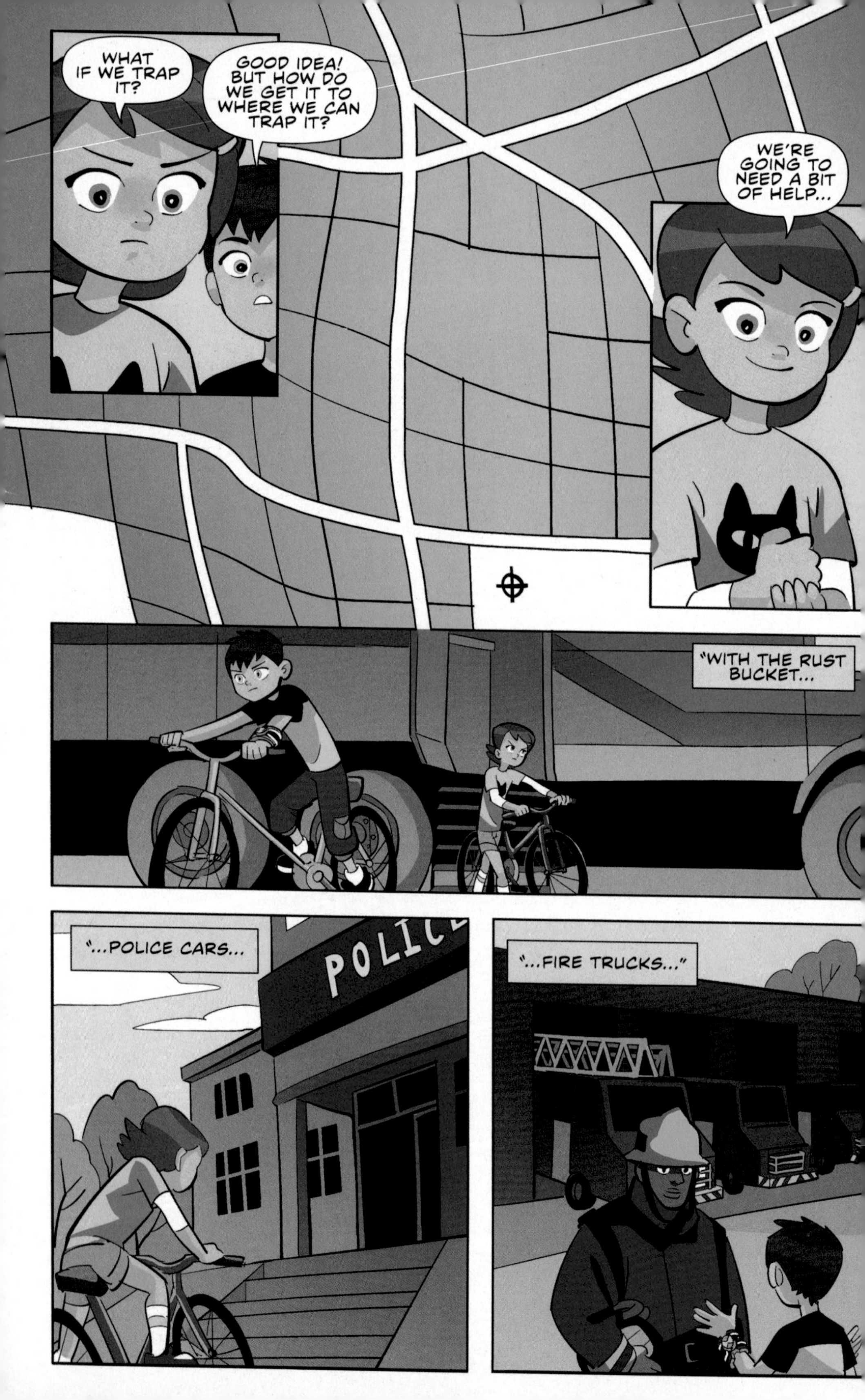

WHAT IF WE TRAP IT?
GOOD IDEA! BUT HOW DO WE GET IT TO WHERE WE CAN TRAP IT?
WE'RE GOING TO NEED A BIT OF HELP...
"WITH THE RUST BUCKET...
"...POLICE CARS...
POLICE
"...FIRE TRUCKS..."

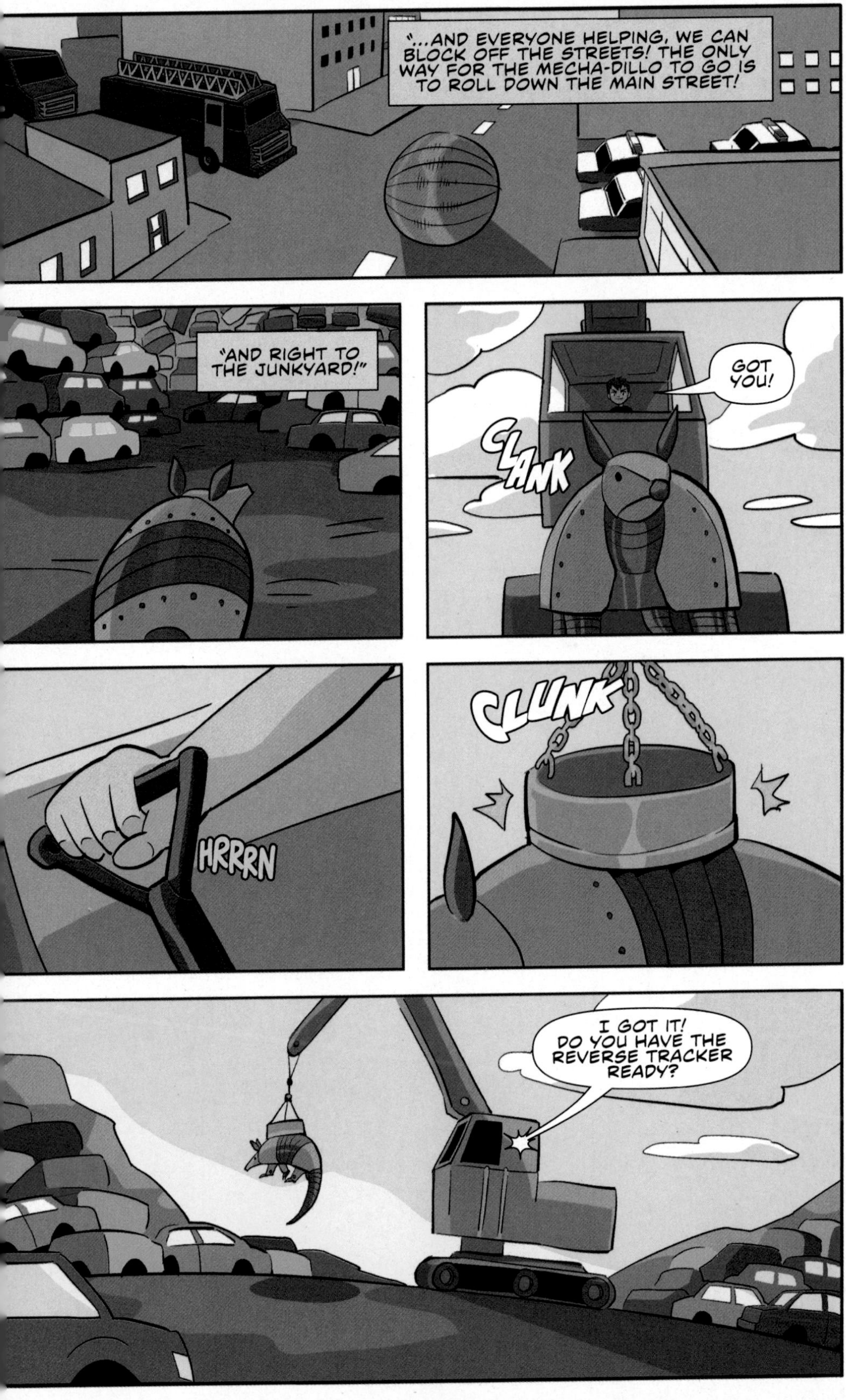
"...AND EVERYONE HELPING, WE CAN BLOCK OFF THE STREETS! THE ONLY WAY FOR THE MECHA-DILLO TO GO IS TO ROLL DOWN THE MAIN STREET!
"AND RIGHT TO THE JUNKYARD!"
GOT YOU!
CLANK
HRRRN
CLUNK
I GOT IT! DO YOU HAVE THE REVERSE TRACKER READY?

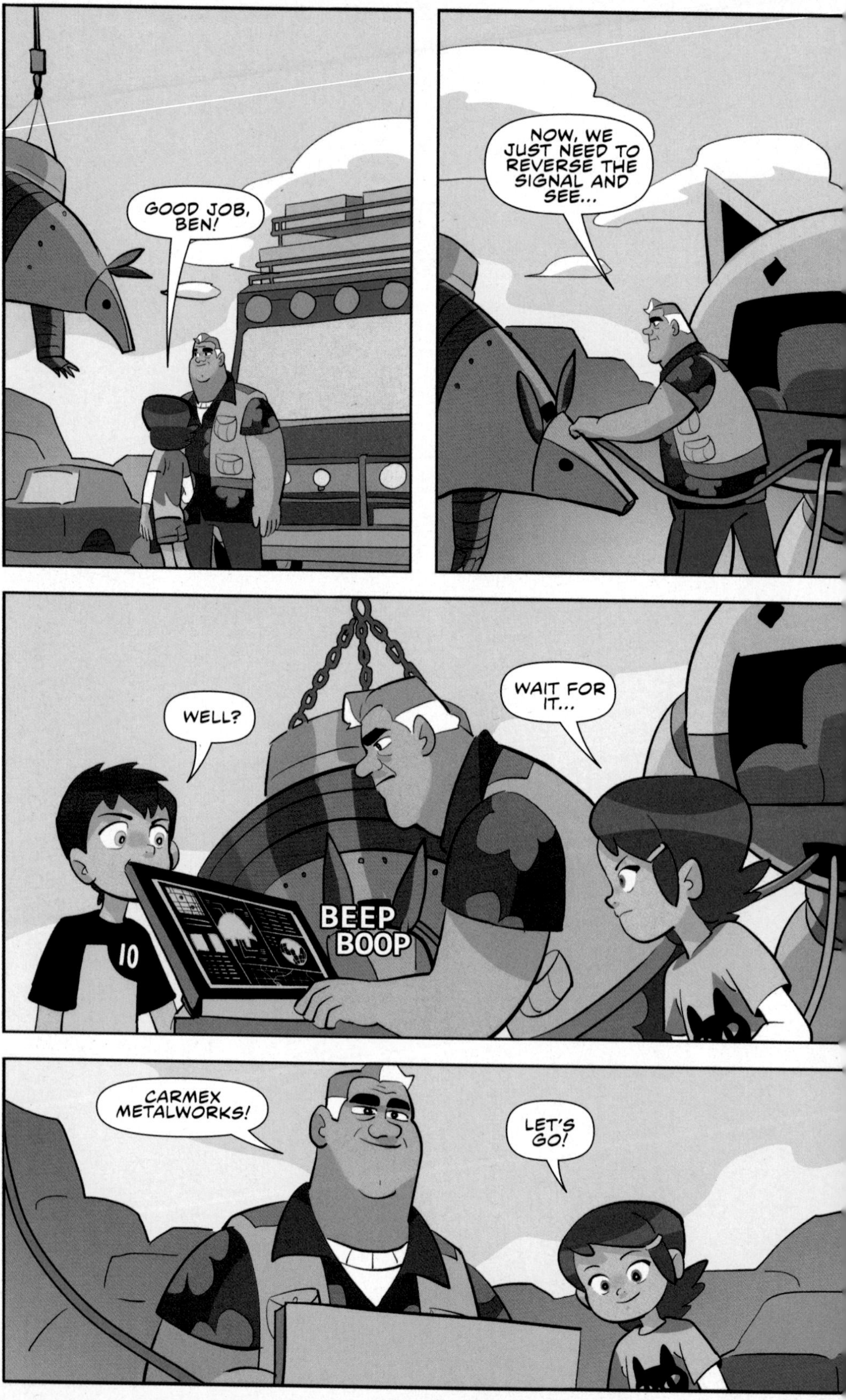
GOOD JOB, BEN!
NOW, WE JUST NEED TO REVERSE THE SIGNAL AND SEE...
WELL?
WAIT FOR IT...
BEEP BOOP
10
CARMEX METALWORKS!
LET'S GO!

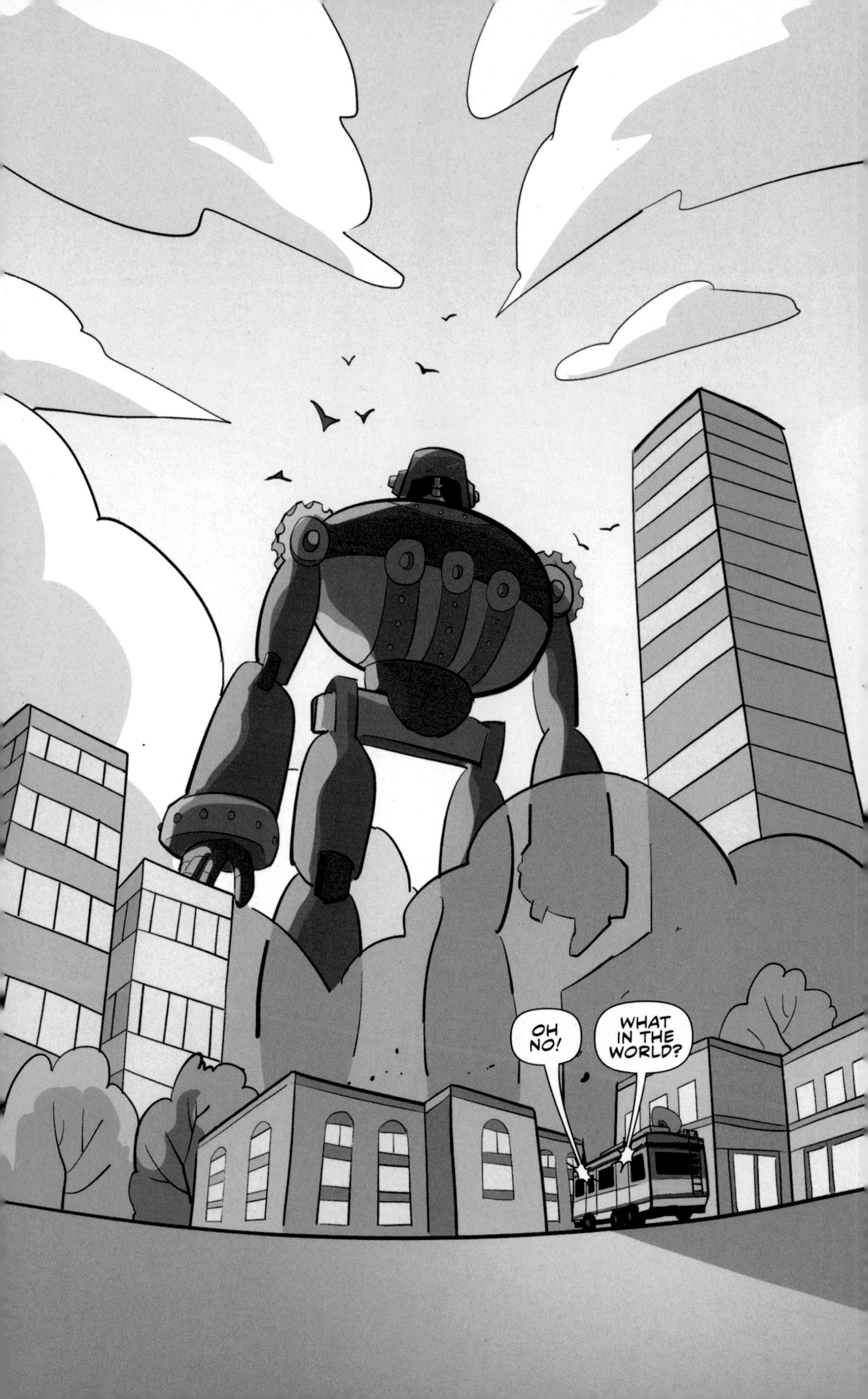
OH NO!
WHAT IN THE WORLD?

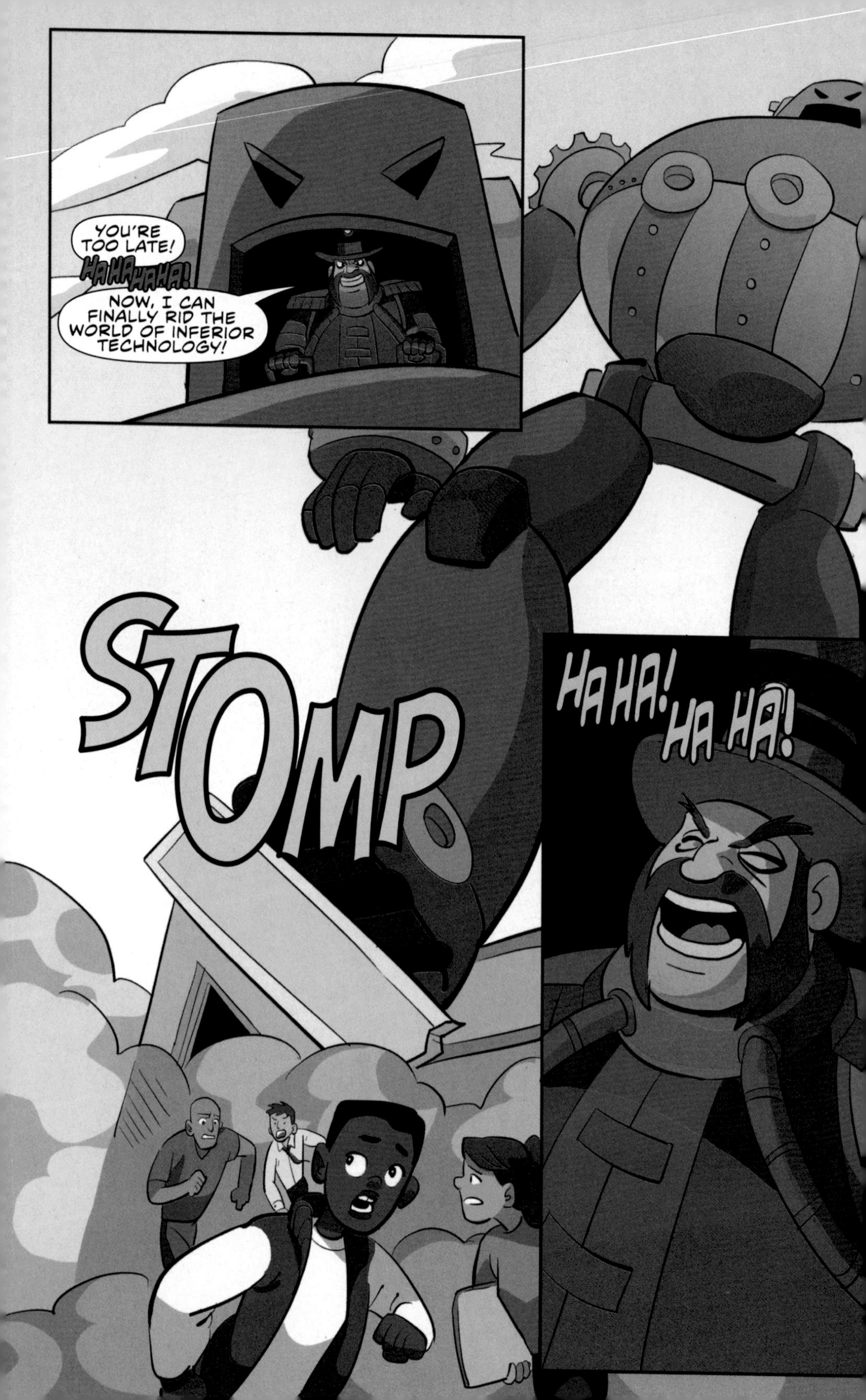
YOU'RE TOO LATE!
HAHAHAHA!
NOW, I CAN FINALLY RID THE WORLD OF INFERIOR TECHNOLOGY!
STOMP
HA HA! HA HA!

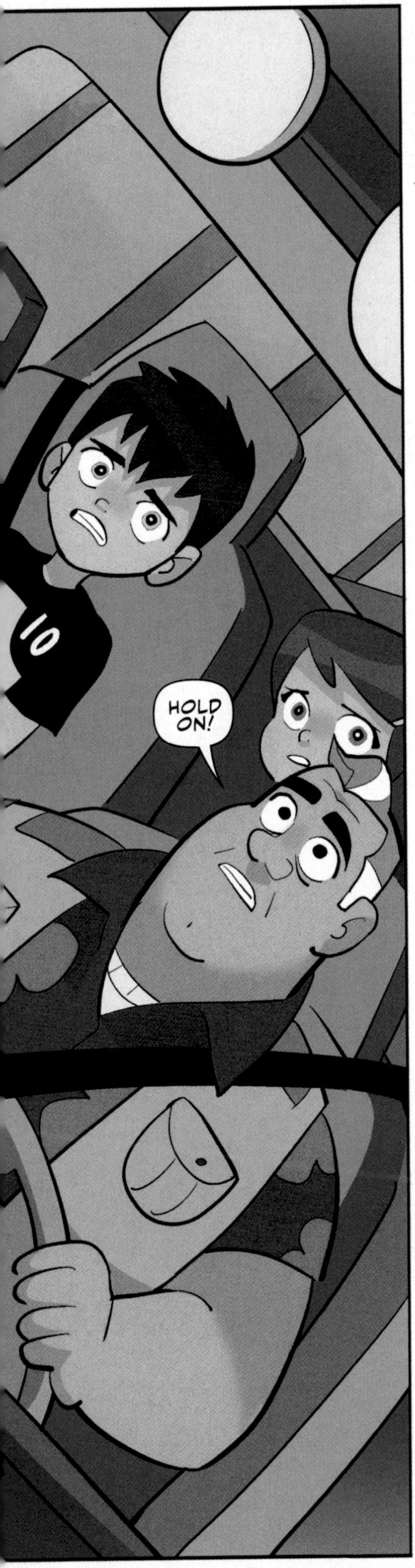
HOLD ON!

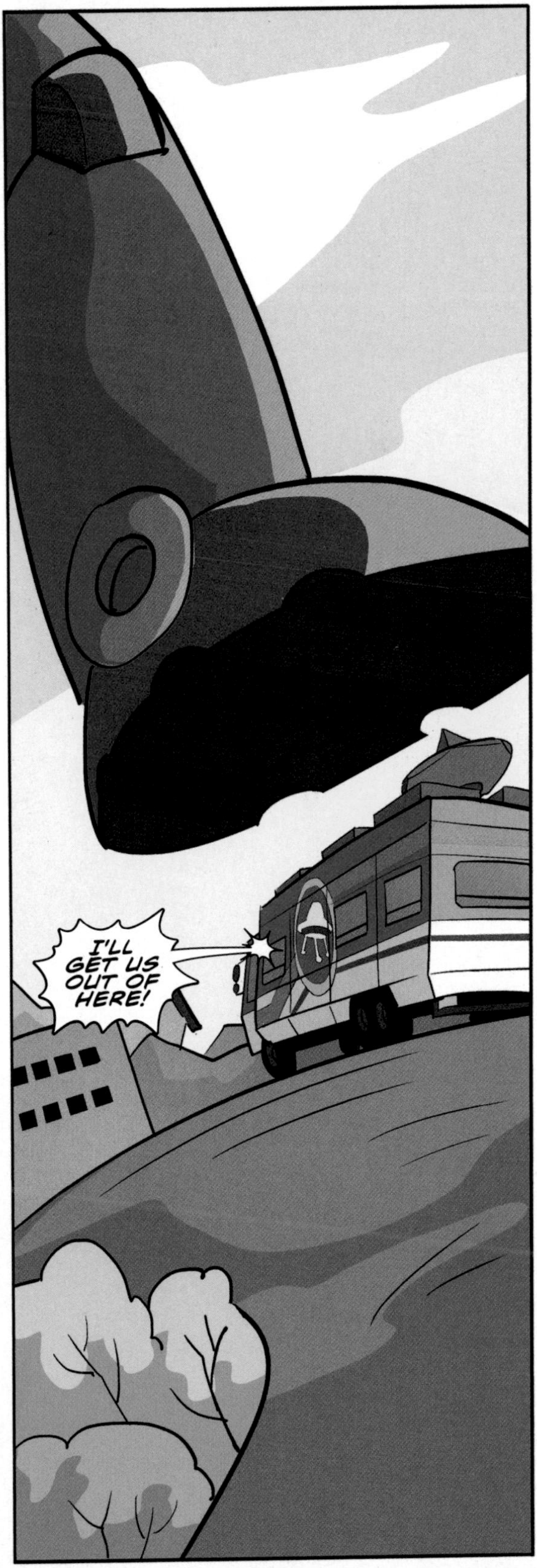
I'LL GET US OUT OF HERE!

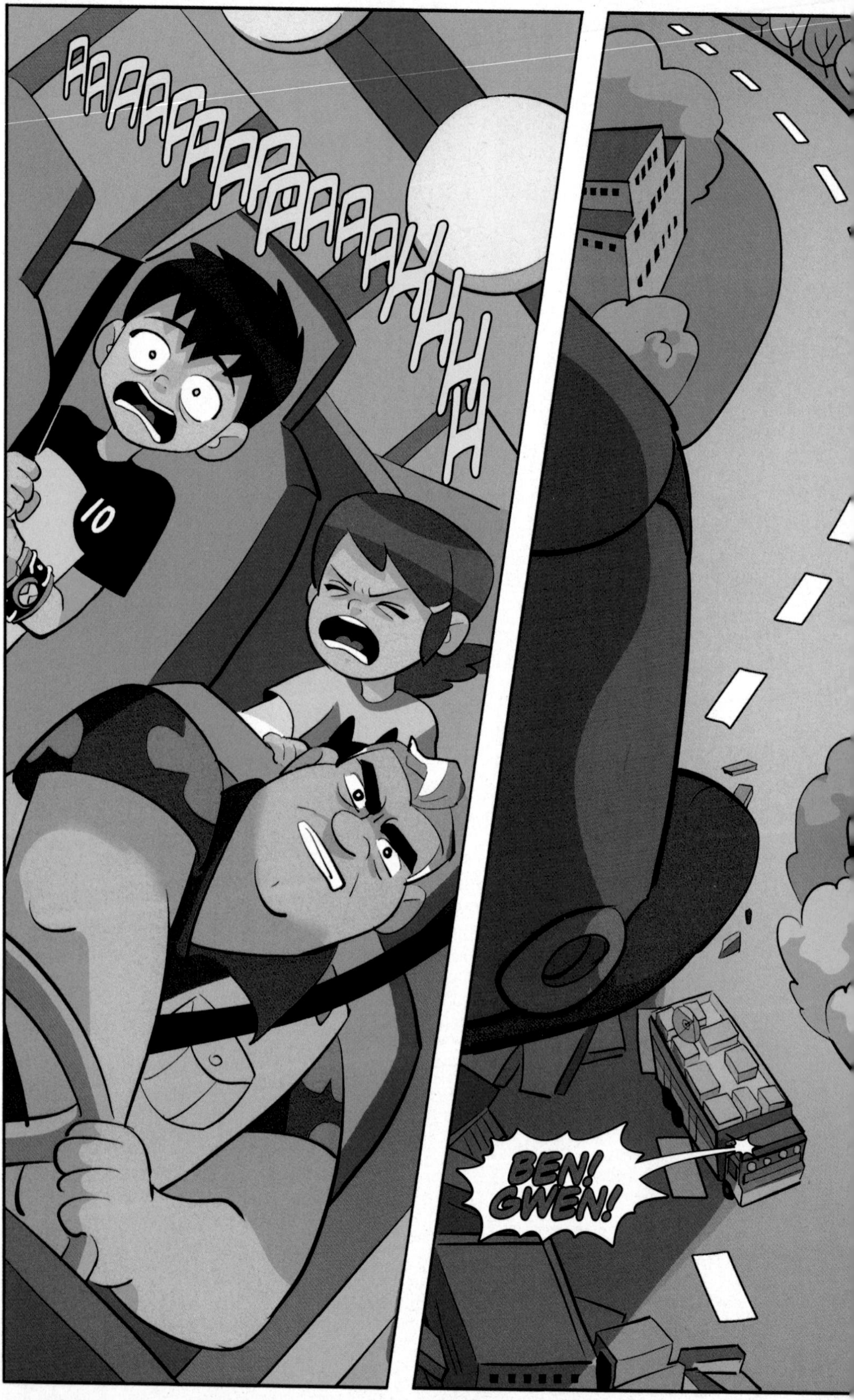
AAAAAAAAAAAAHHHH
BEN! GWEN!

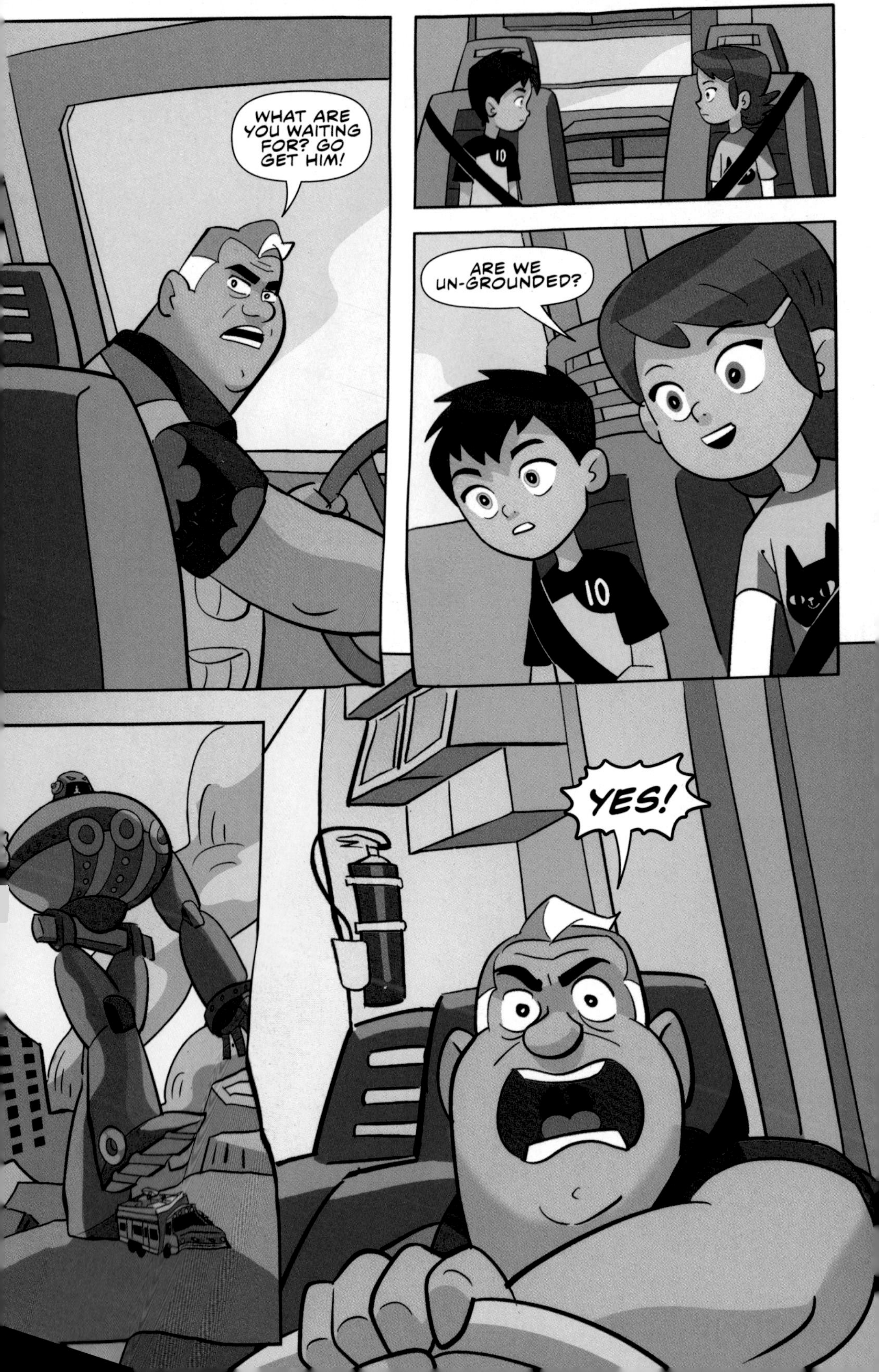
WHAT ARE YOU WAITING FOR? GO GET HIM!
ARE WE UN-GROUNDED?
YES!

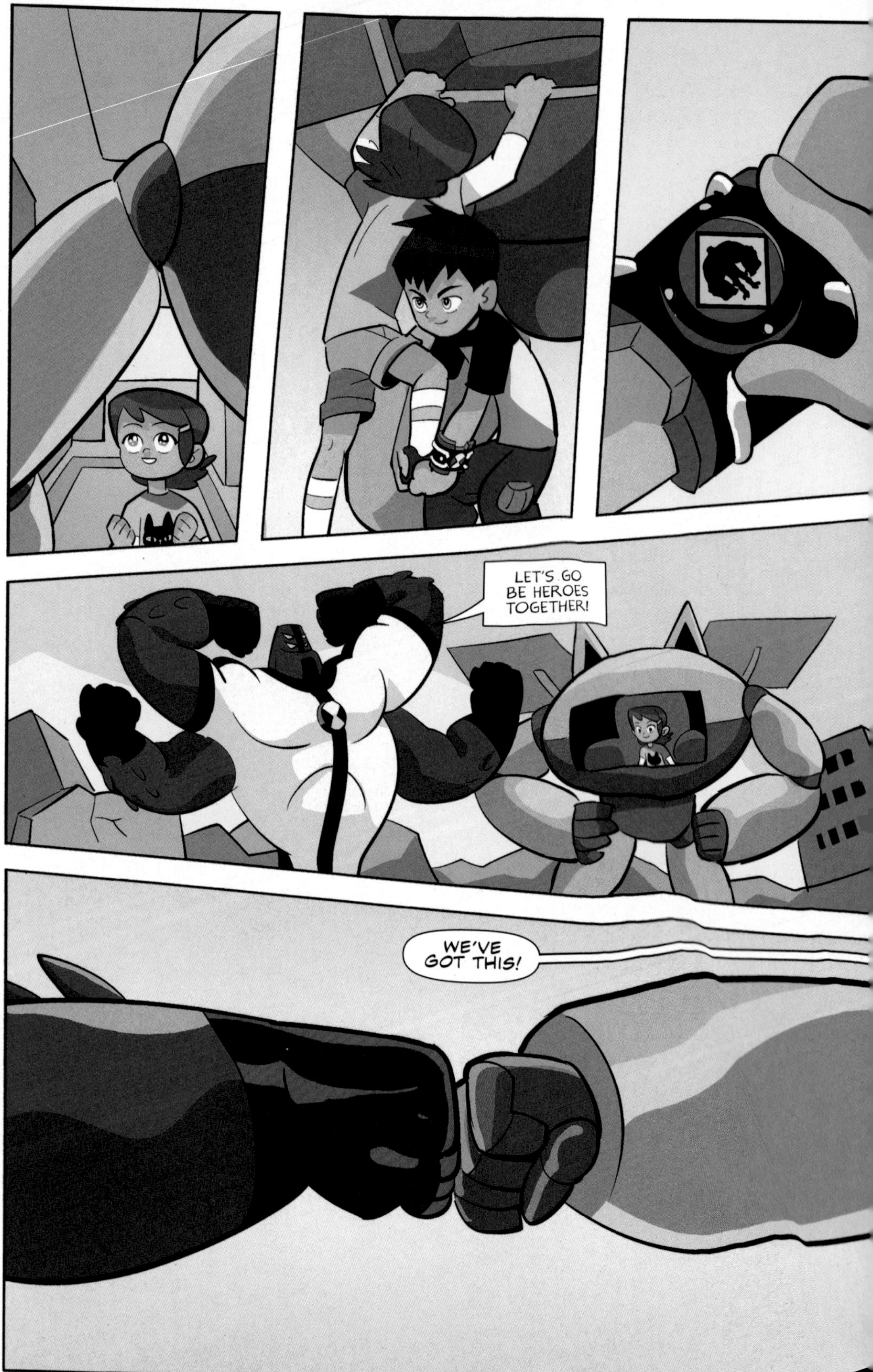
LET'S GO
BE HEROES
TOGETHER!
WE'VE
GOT THIS!

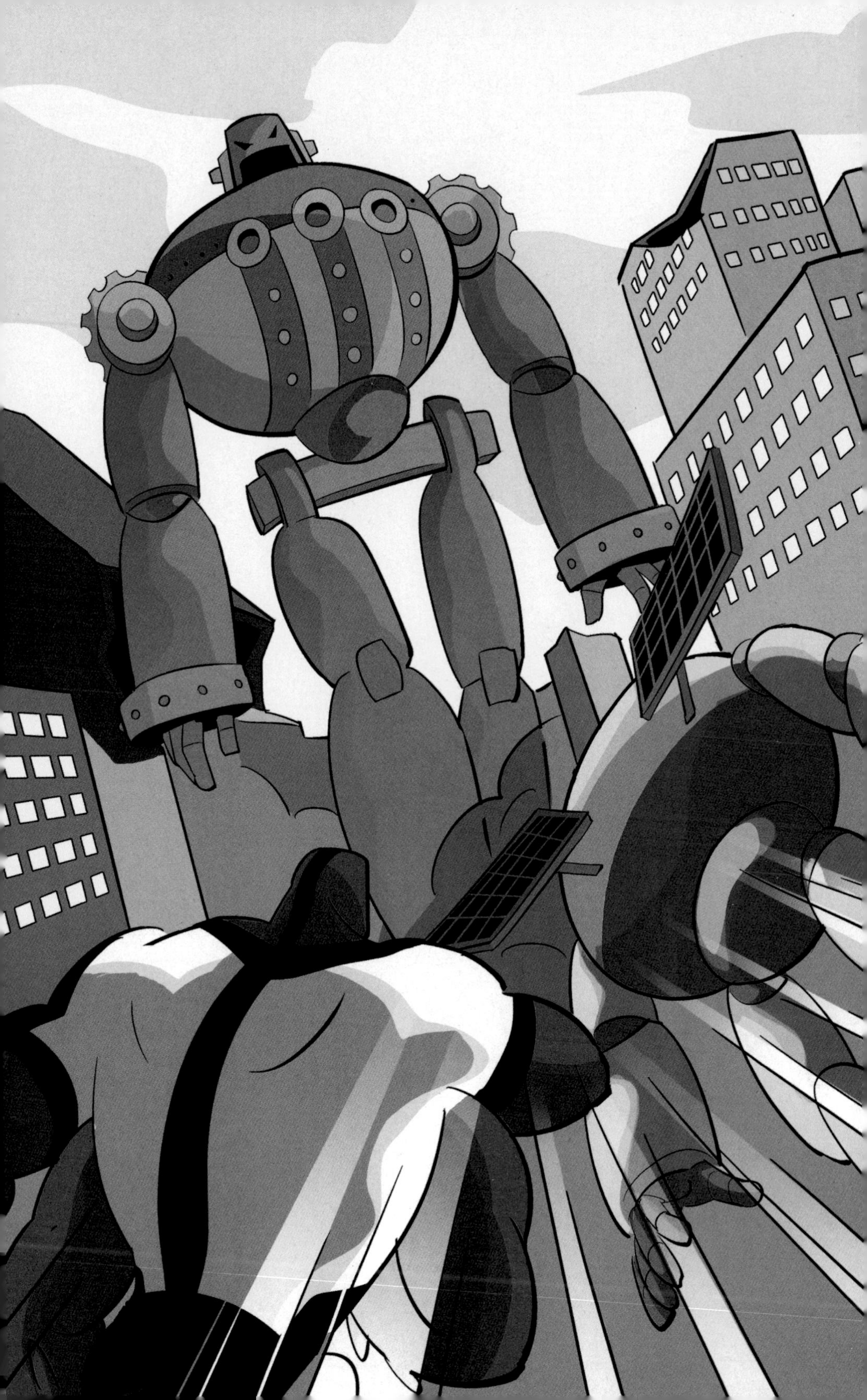

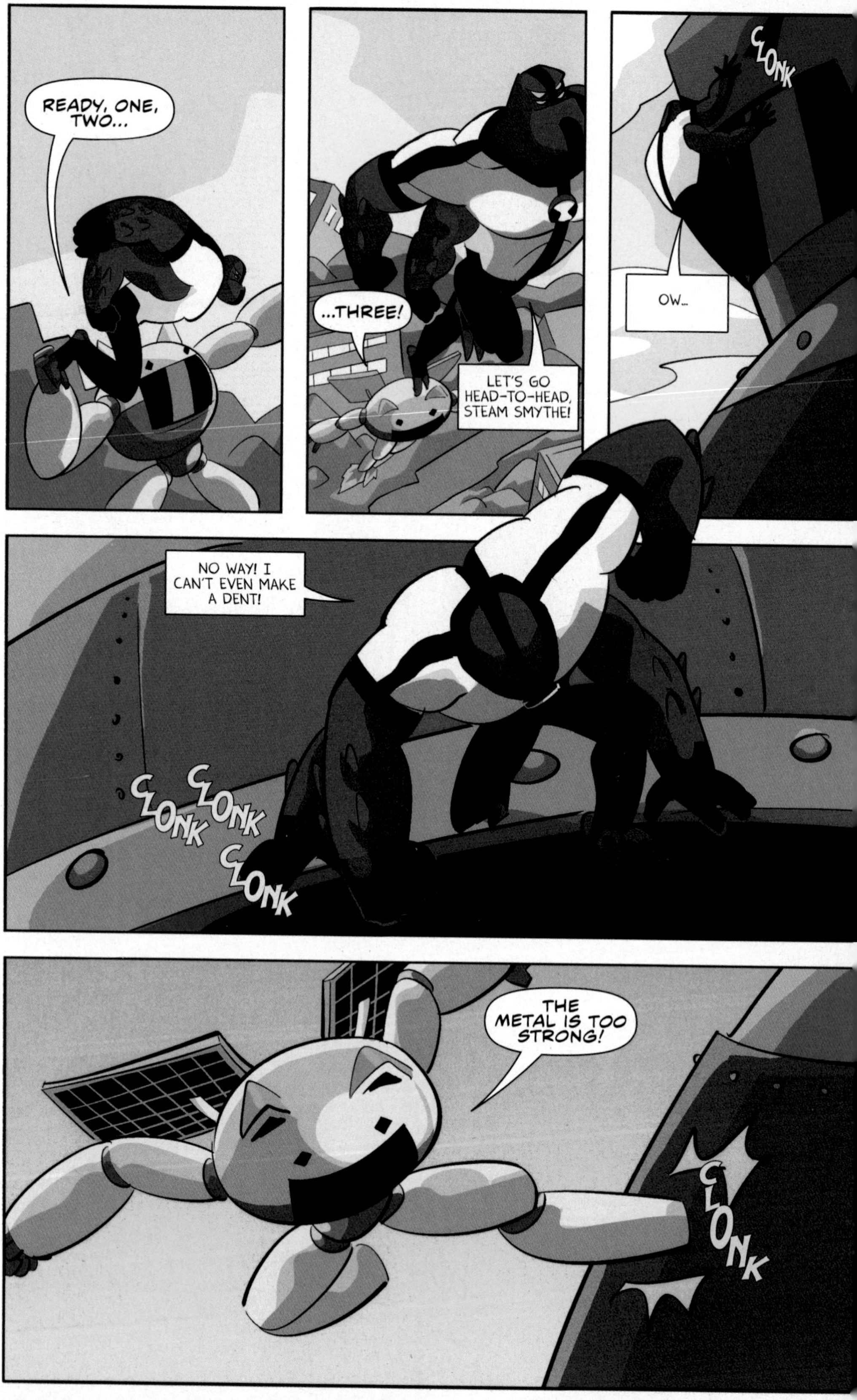
READY, ONE, TWO...
...THREE!
LET'S GO HEAD-TO-HEAD, STEAM SMYTHE!
CLONK
OW...
NO WAY! I CAN'T EVEN MAKE A DENT!
CLONK
CLONK
CLONK
THE METAL IS TOO STRONG!
CLONK

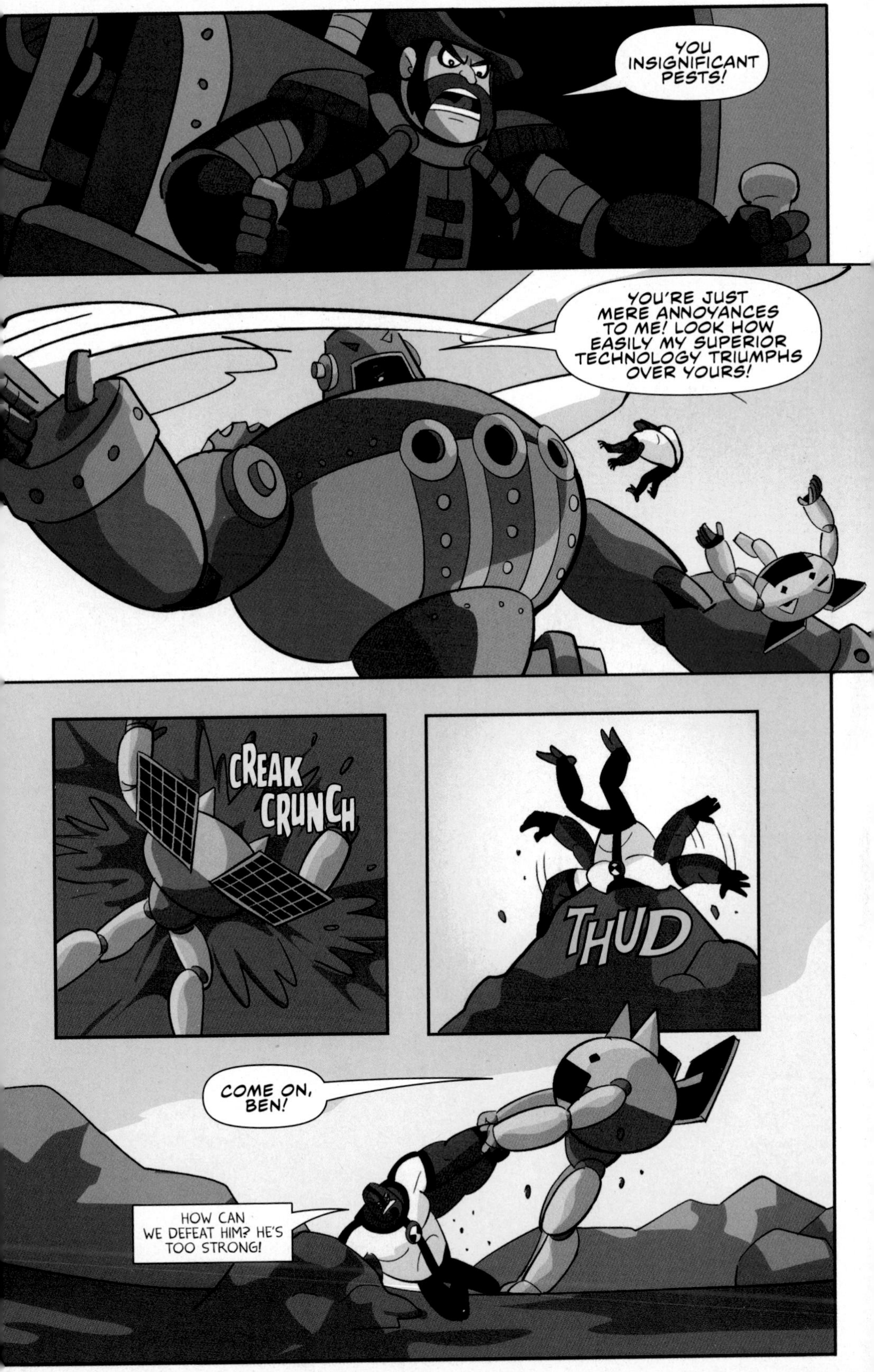
YOU INSIGNIFICANT PESTS!
YOU'RE JUST MERE ANNOYANCES TO ME! LOOK HOW EASILY MY SUPERIOR TECHNOLOGY TRIUMPHS OVER YOURS!
CREAK
CRUNCH
THUD
COME ON, BEN!
HOW CAN WE DEFEAT HIM? HE'S TOO STRONG!

CAN YOU TRY YOUR HEAT-VISION?

YEAH!

HAHA! AS YOU CAN SEE, I'VE IMPROVED UPON MY ORIGINAL DESIGN!

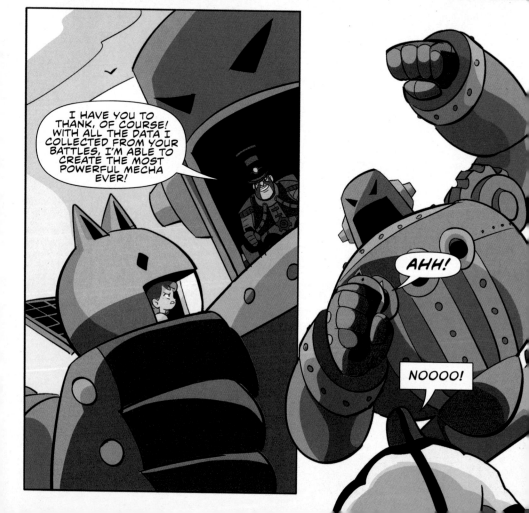

I HAVE YOU TO THANK, OF COURSE! WITH ALL THE DATA I COLLECTED FROM YOUR BATTLES, I'M ABLE TO CREATE THE MOST POWERFUL MECHA EVER!

AHH!

NOOOO!

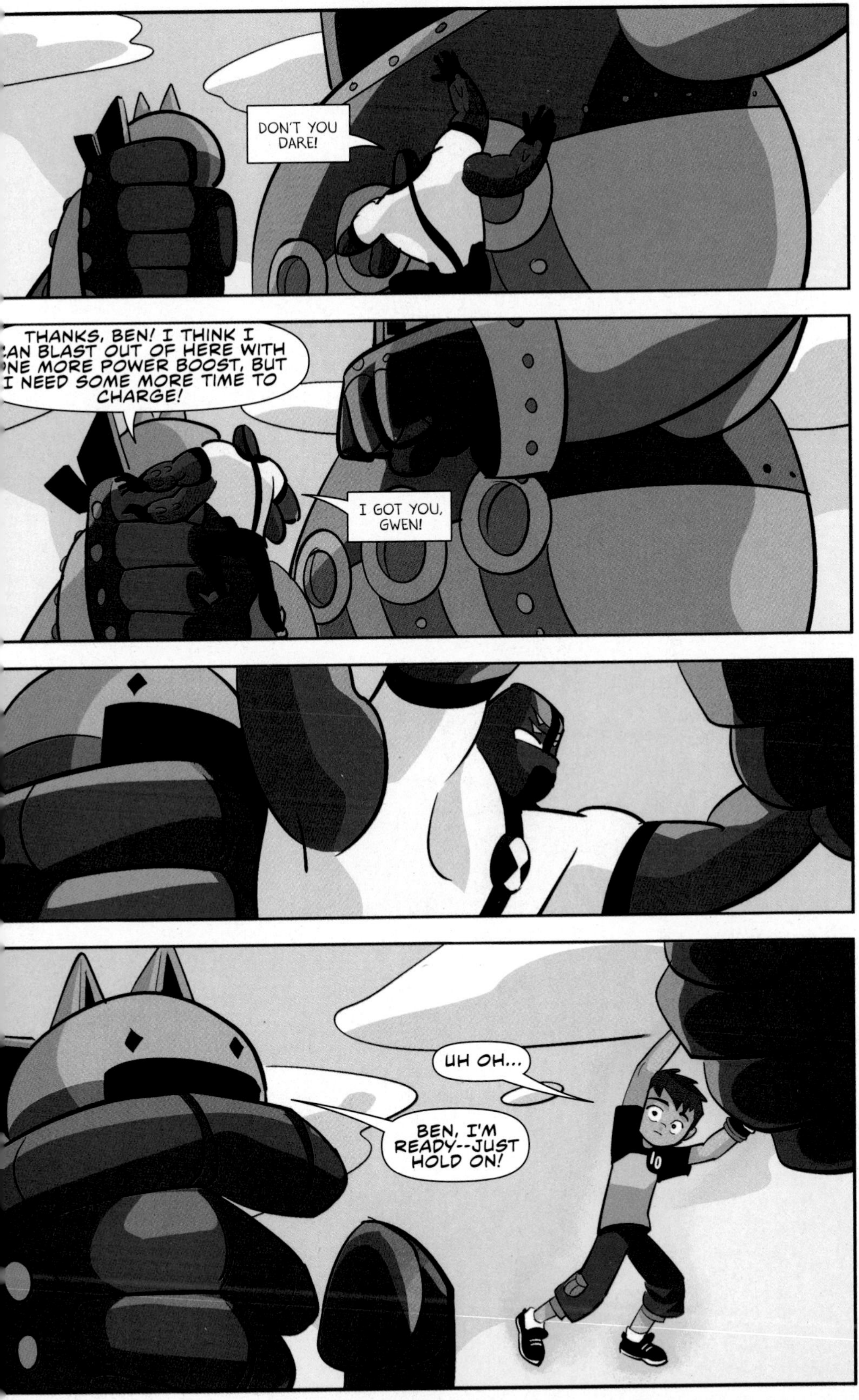
DON'T YOU DARE!
THANKS, BEN! I THINK I CAN BLAST OUT OF HERE WITH ONE MORE POWER BOOST, BUT I NEED SOME MORE TIME TO CHARGE!
I GOT YOU, GWEN!
UH OH...
BEN, I'M READY--JUST HOLD ON!
10

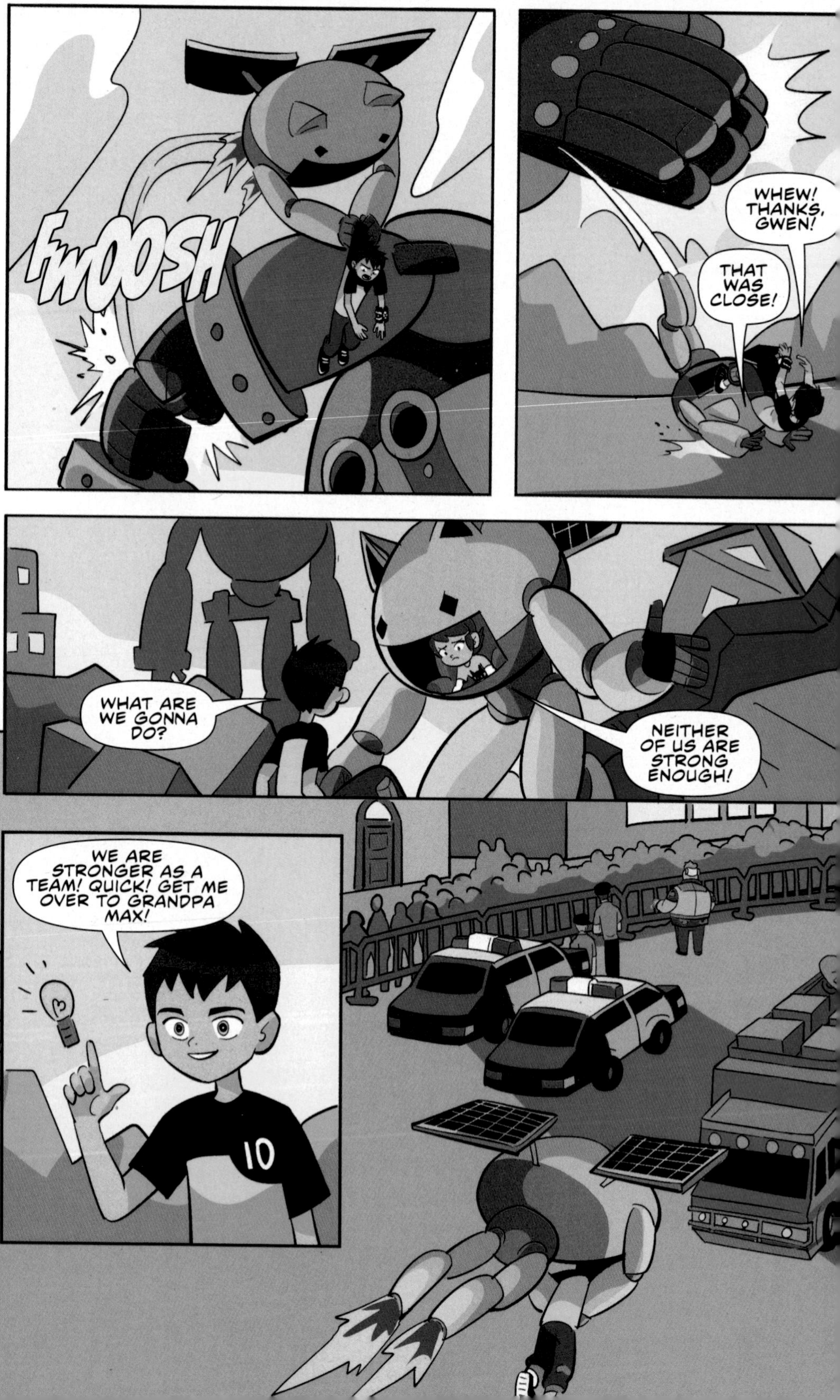
FWOOSH
WHEW! THANKS, GWEN!
THAT WAS CLOSE!
WHAT ARE WE GONNA DO?
NEITHER OF US ARE STRONG ENOUGH!
WE ARE STRONGER AS A TEAM! QUICK! GET ME OVER TO GRANDPA MAX!
10

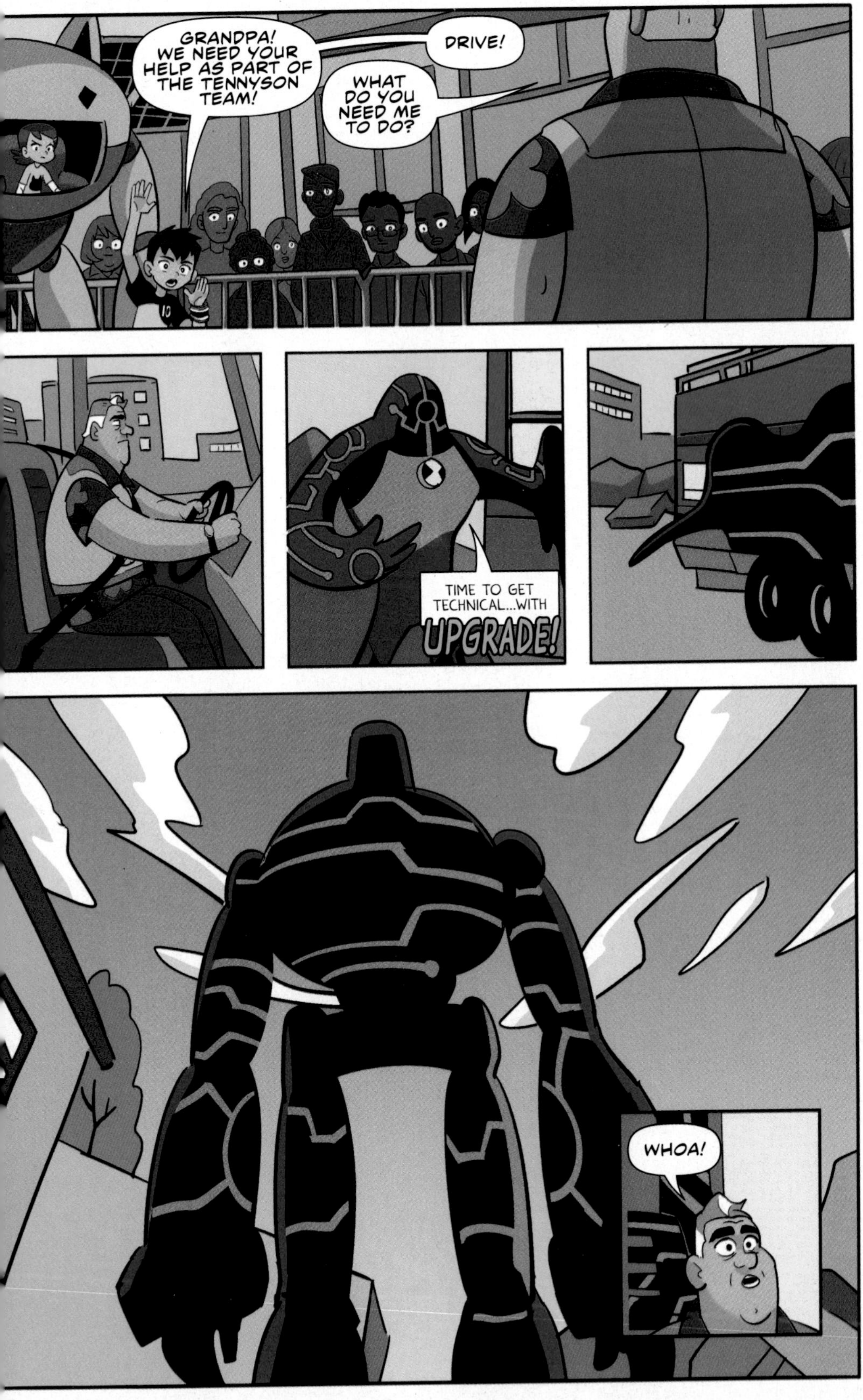
GRANDPA! WE NEED YOUR HELP AS PART OF THE TENNYSON TEAM!
WHAT DO YOU NEED ME TO DO?
DRIVE!
TIME TO GET TECHNICAL...WITH
UPGRADE!
WHOA!

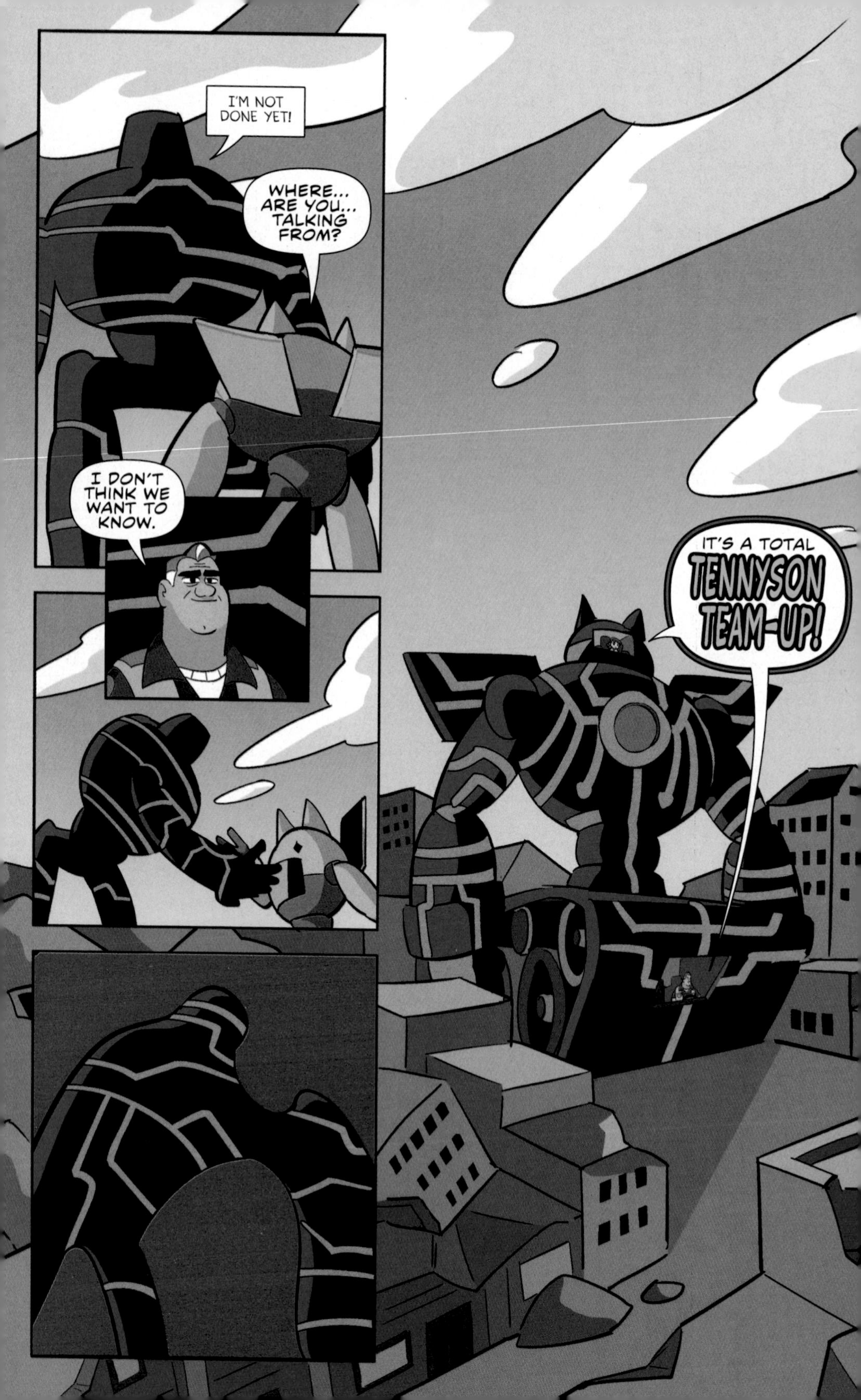
I'M NOT DONE YET!
WHERE... ARE YOU... TALKING FROM?
I DON'T THINK WE WANT TO KNOW.
IT'S A TOTAL TENNYSON TEAM-UP!

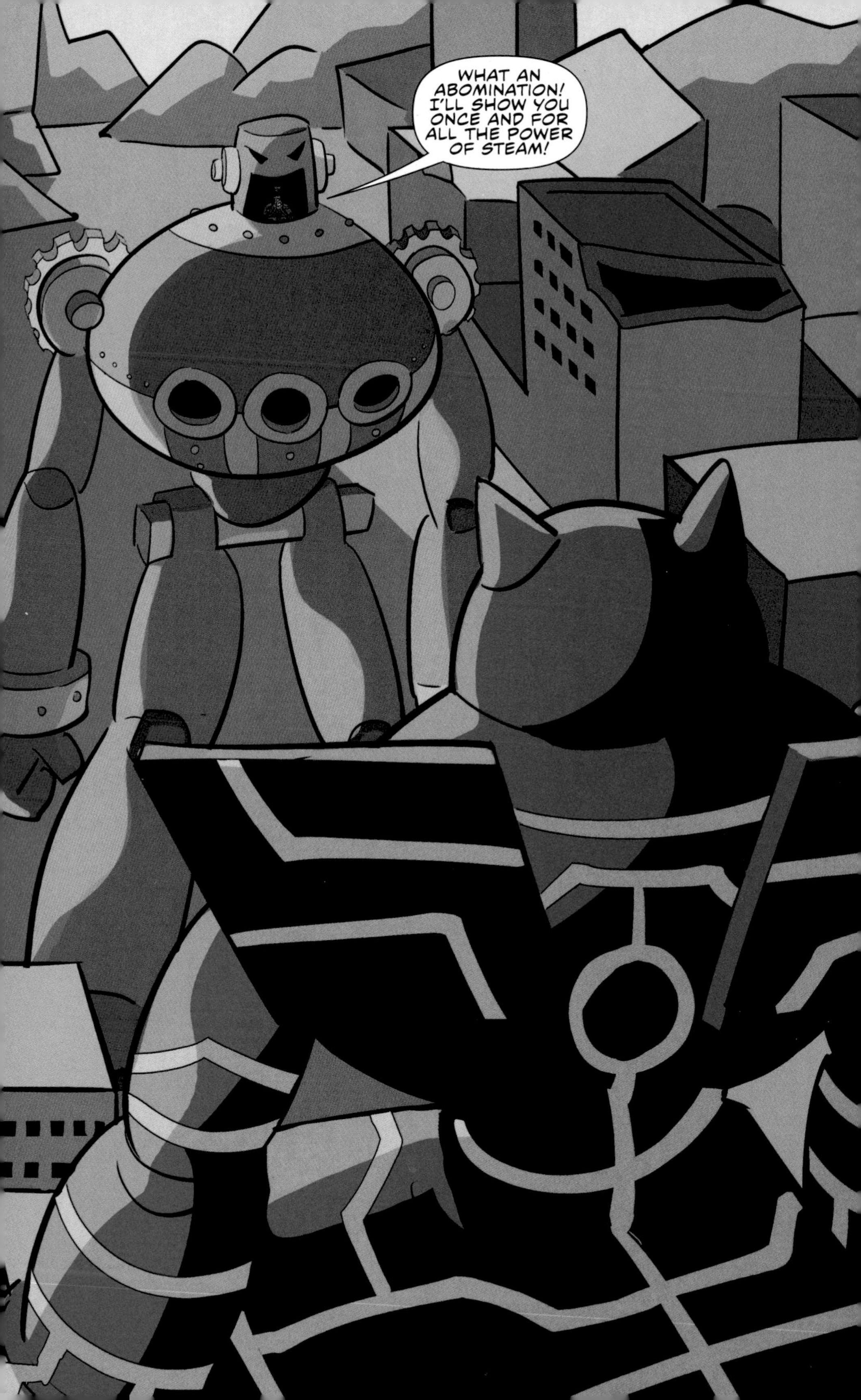
WHAT AN ABOMINATION! I'LL SHOW YOU ONCE AND FOR ALL THE POWER OF STEAM!

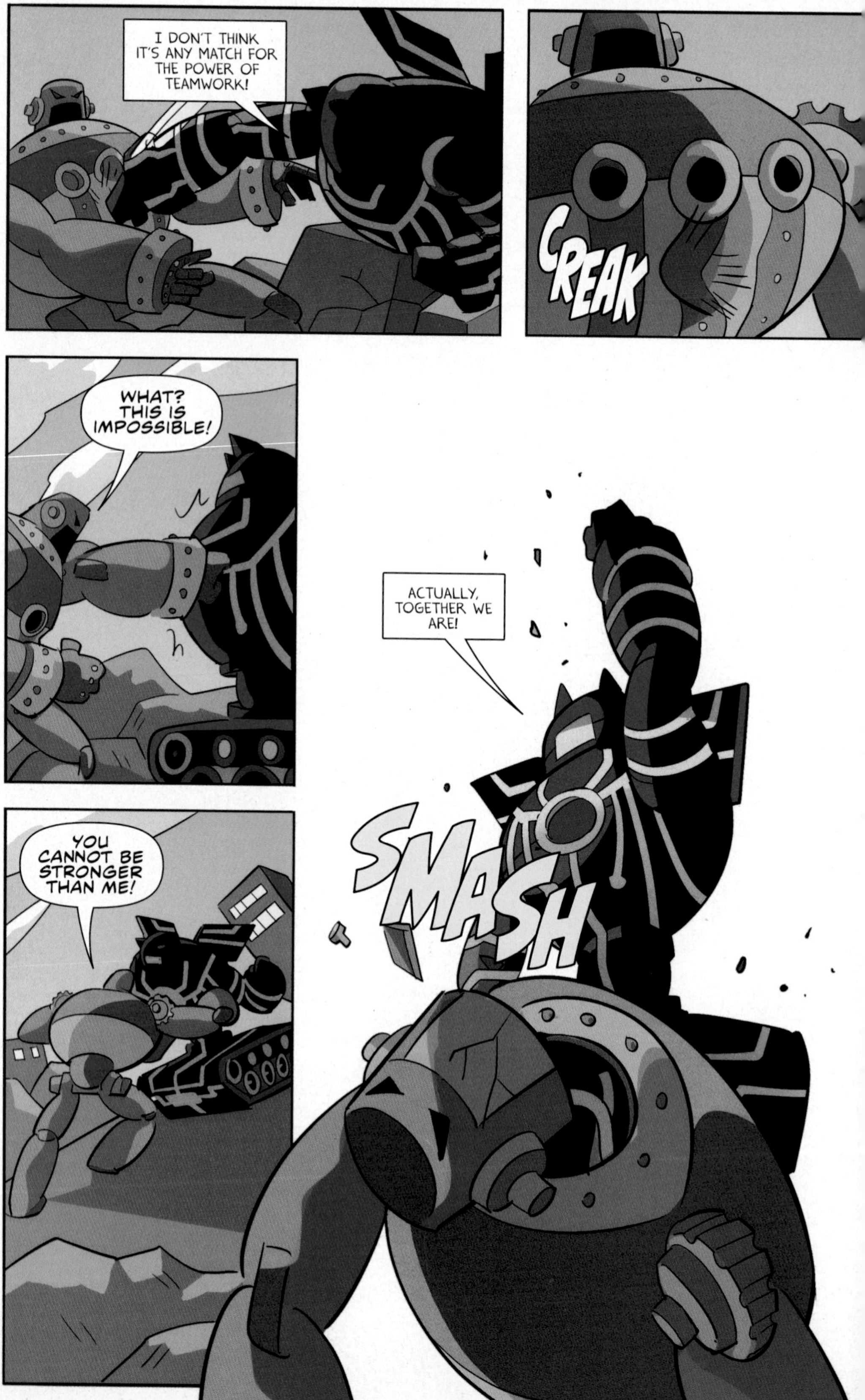
I DON'T THINK IT'S ANY MATCH FOR THE POWER OF TEAMWORK!
CREAK
WHAT? THIS IS IMPOSSIBLE!
YOU CANNOT BE STRONGER THAN ME!
ACTUALLY, TOGETHER WE ARE!
SMASH

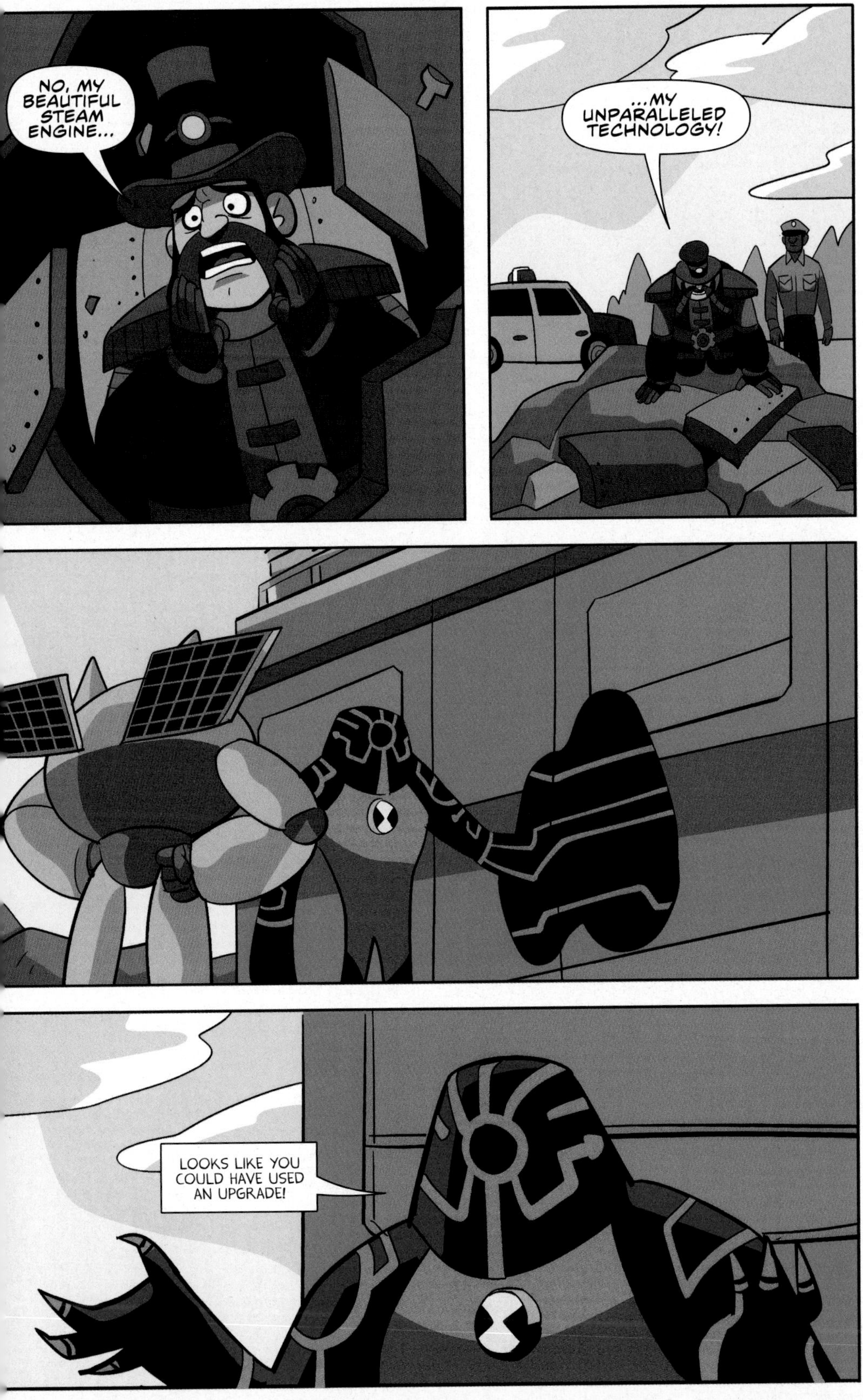
NO, MY BEAUTIFUL STEAM ENGINE...
...MY UNPARALLELED TECHNOLOGY!
LOOKS LIKE YOU COULD HAVE USED AN UPGRADE!

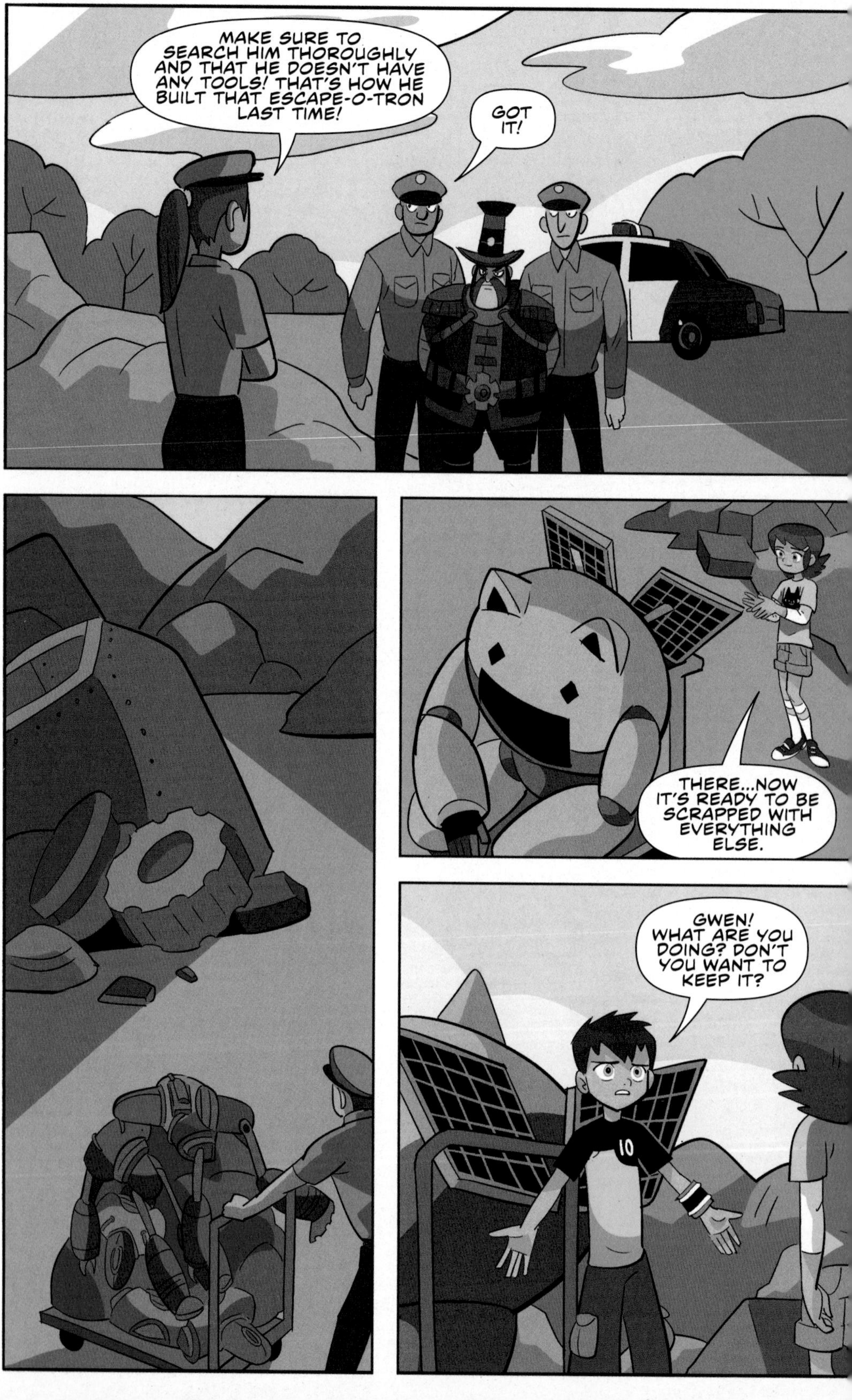
MAKE SURE TO SEARCH HIM THOROUGHLY AND THAT HE DOESN'T HAVE ANY TOOLS! THAT'S HOW HE BUILT THAT ESCAPE-O-TRON LAST TIME!
GOT IT!
THERE...NOW IT'S READY TO BE SCRAPPED WITH EVERYTHING ELSE.
GWEN! WHAT ARE YOU DOING? DON'T YOU WANT TO KEEP IT?
10

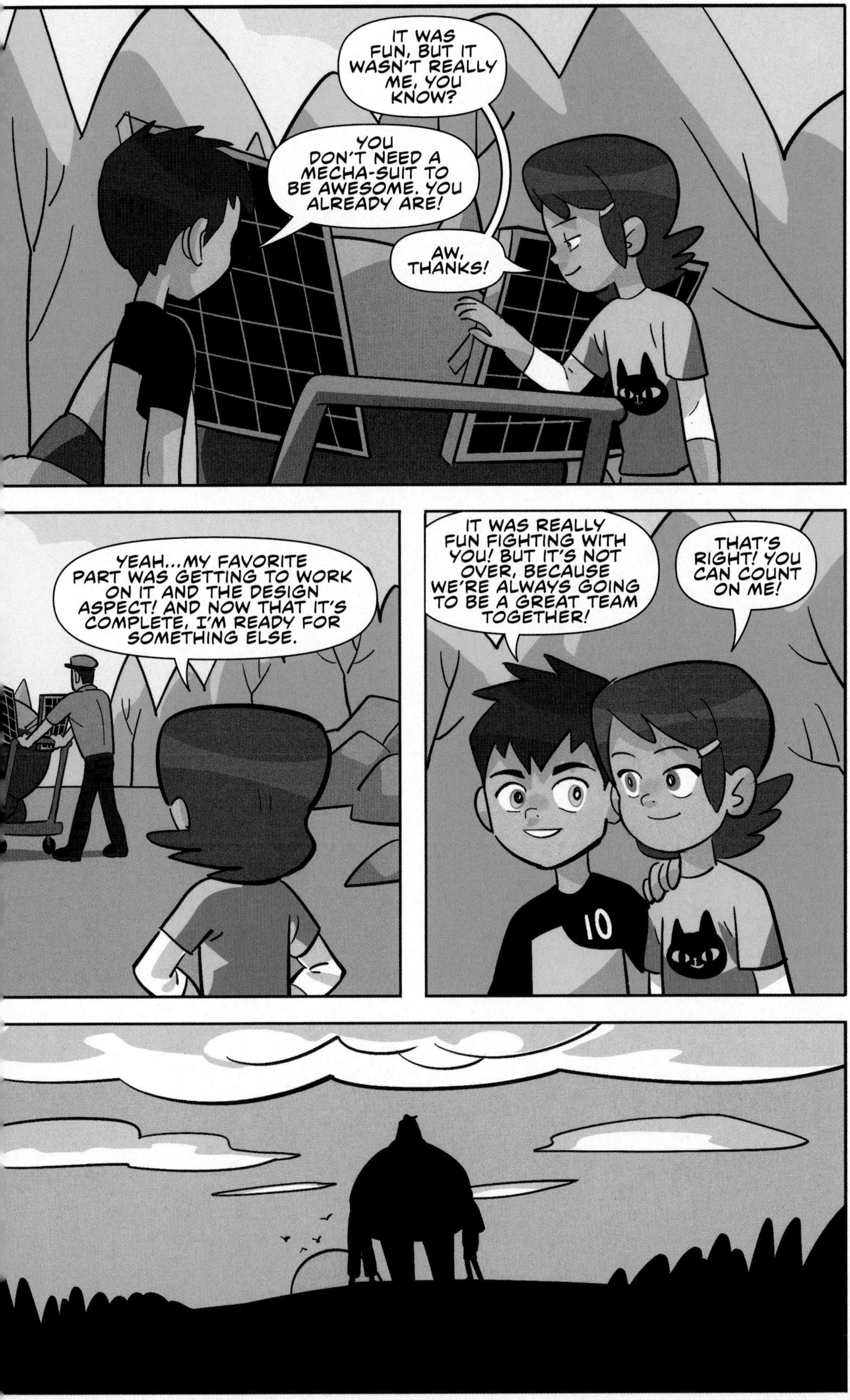
IT WAS FUN, BUT IT WASN'T REALLY ME, YOU KNOW?
YOU DON'T NEED A MECHA-SUIT TO BE AWESOME. YOU ALREADY ARE!
AW, THANKS!
YEAH...MY FAVORITE PART WAS GETTING TO WORK ON IT AND THE DESIGN ASPECT! AND NOW THAT IT'S COMPLETE, I'M READY FOR SOMETHING ELSE.
IT WAS REALLY FUN FIGHTING WITH YOU! BUT IT'S NOT OVER, BECAUSE WE'RE ALWAYS GOING TO BE A GREAT TEAM TOGETHER!
THAT'S RIGHT! YOU CAN COUNT ON ME!
10

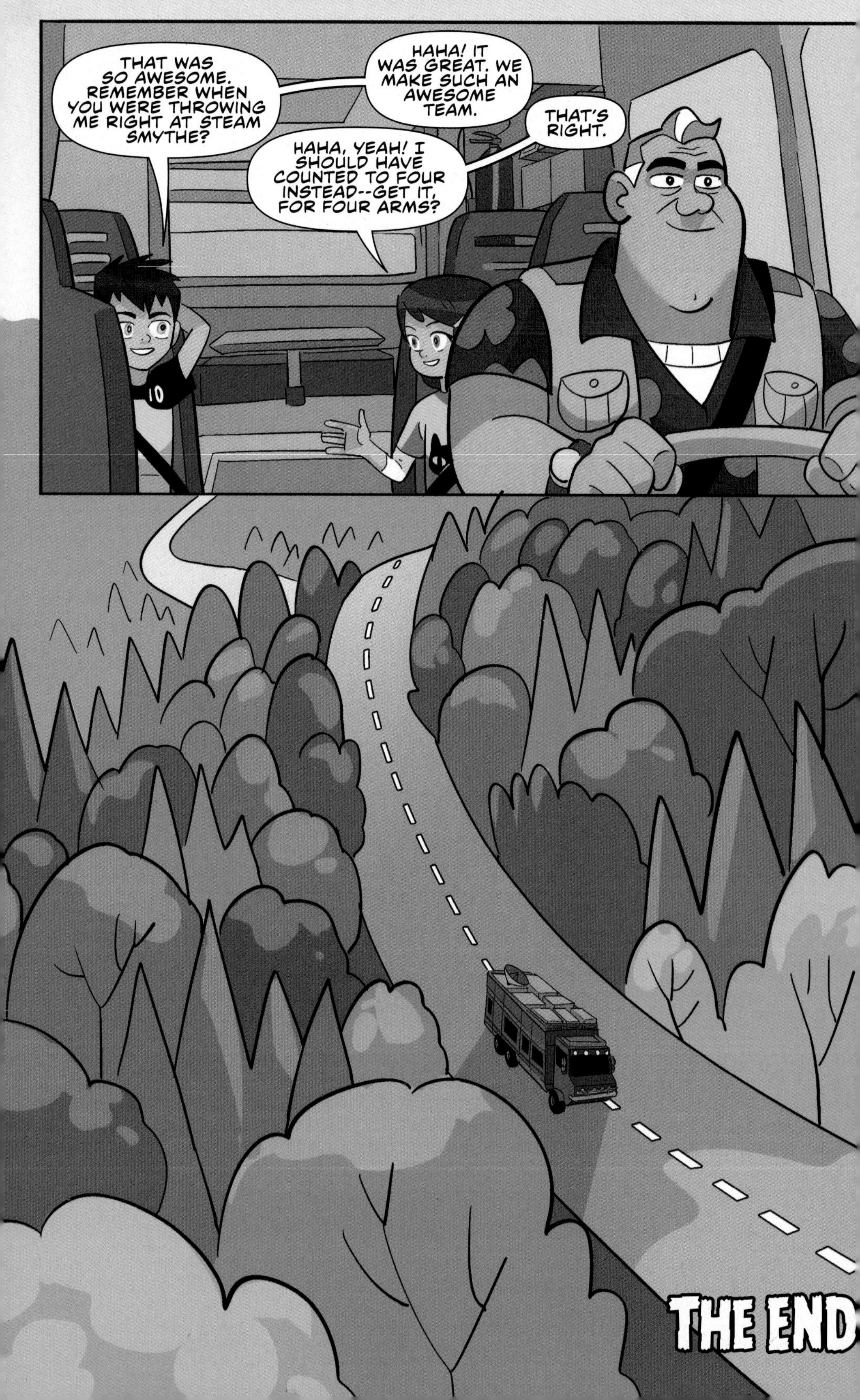
THAT WAS SO AWESOME. REMEMBER WHEN YOU WERE THROWING ME RIGHT AT STEAM SMYTHE?
HAHA! IT WAS GREAT. WE MAKE SUCH AN AWESOME TEAM.
HAHA, YEAH! I SHOULD HAVE COUNTED TO FOUR INSTEAD--GET IT, FOR FOUR ARMS?
THAT'S RIGHT.
THE END

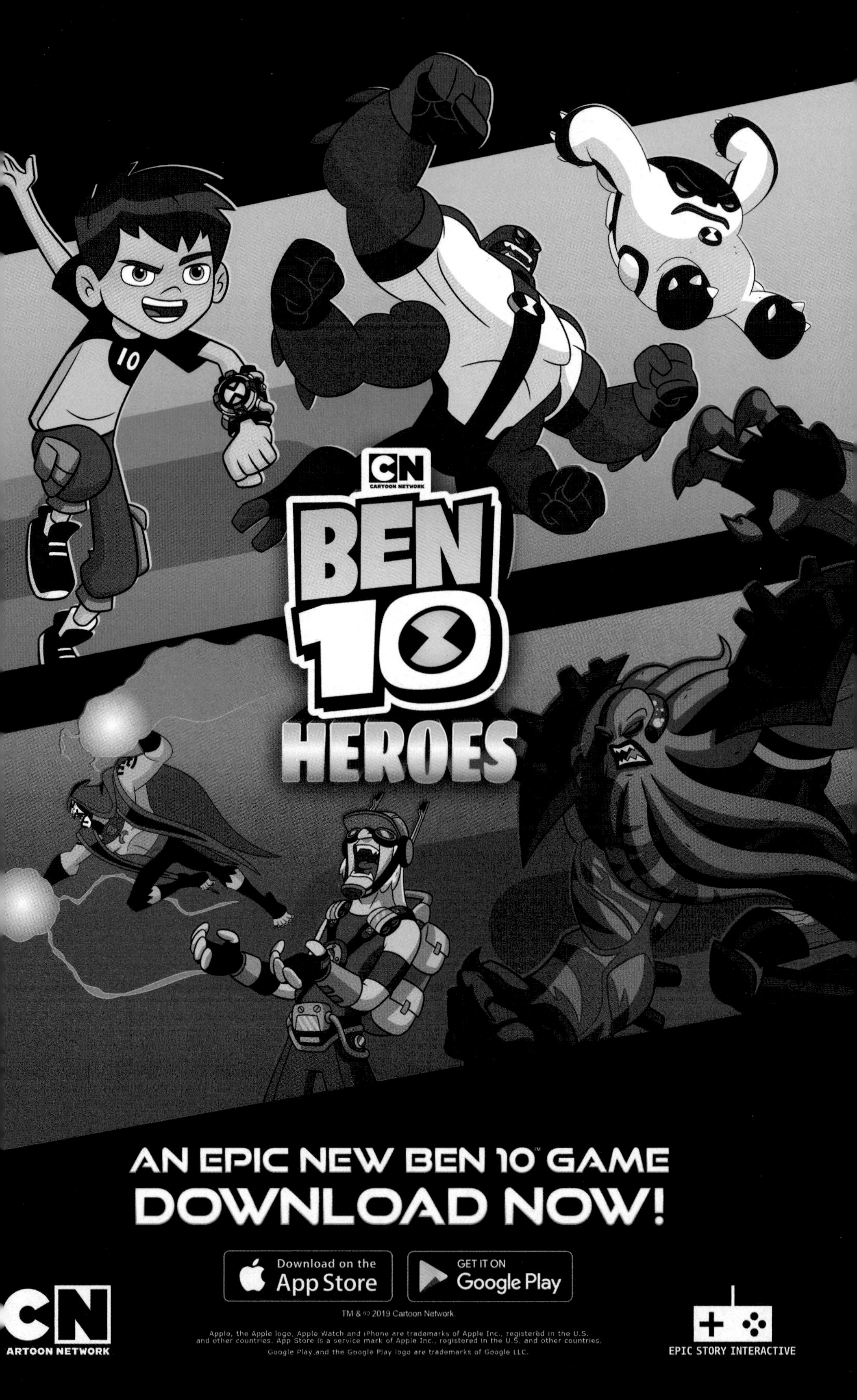
CN
CARTOON NETWORK
BEN 10
HEROES
AN EPIC NEW BEN 10™ GAME
DOWNLOAD NOW!
Download on the App Store
GET IT ON Google Play
TM & © 2019 Cartoon Network.
Apple, the Apple logo, Apple Watch and iPhone are trademarks of Apple Inc., registered in the U.S. and other countries. App Store is a service mark of Apple Inc., registered in the U.S. and other countries.
Google Play and the Google Play logo are trademarks of Google LLC.
ARTOON NETWORK
EPIC STORY INTERACTIVE

BEN'S ADVENTURES IN THE RUSTBUCKET CONTINUE IN...

"THE MANCHESTER MYSTERY"

AVAILABLE SPRING 2020

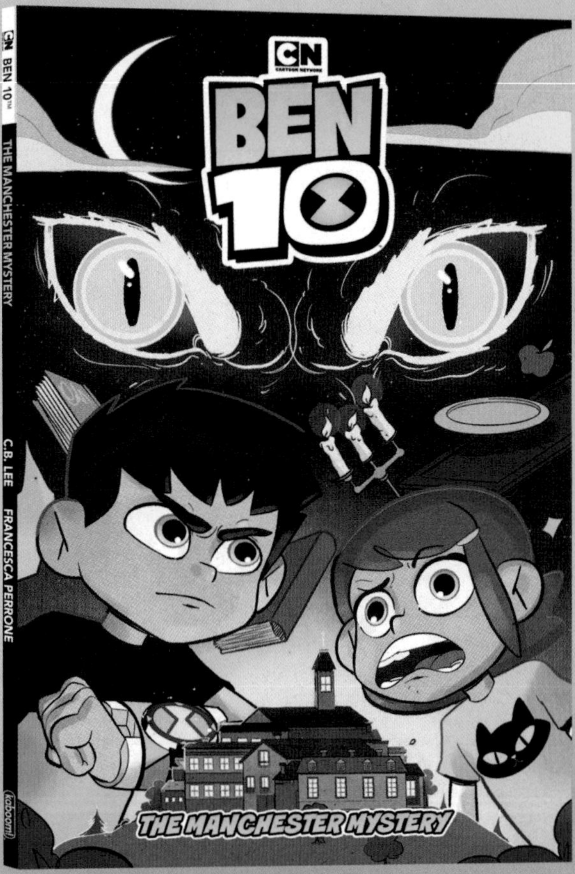
CN CARTOON NETWORK
BEN 10
THE MANCHESTER MYSTERY
BEN 10™
THE MANCHESTER MYSTERY
C.B. LEE
FRANCESCA PERRONE
kaboom!

WRITTEN BY

C.B. LEE

ILLUSTRATED BY

FRANCESCA PERRONE

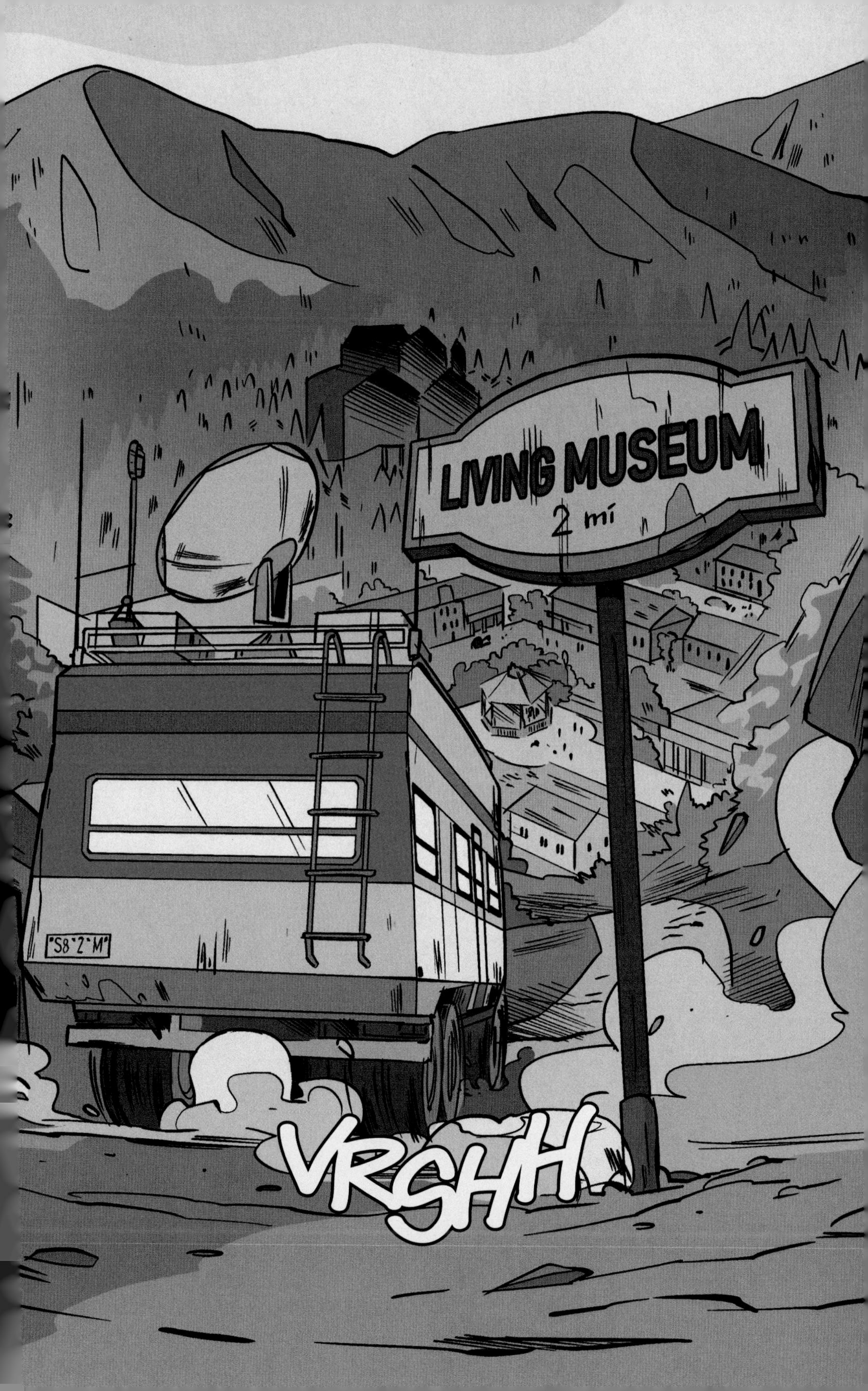
LIVING MUSEUM
2 mi
VRGHH

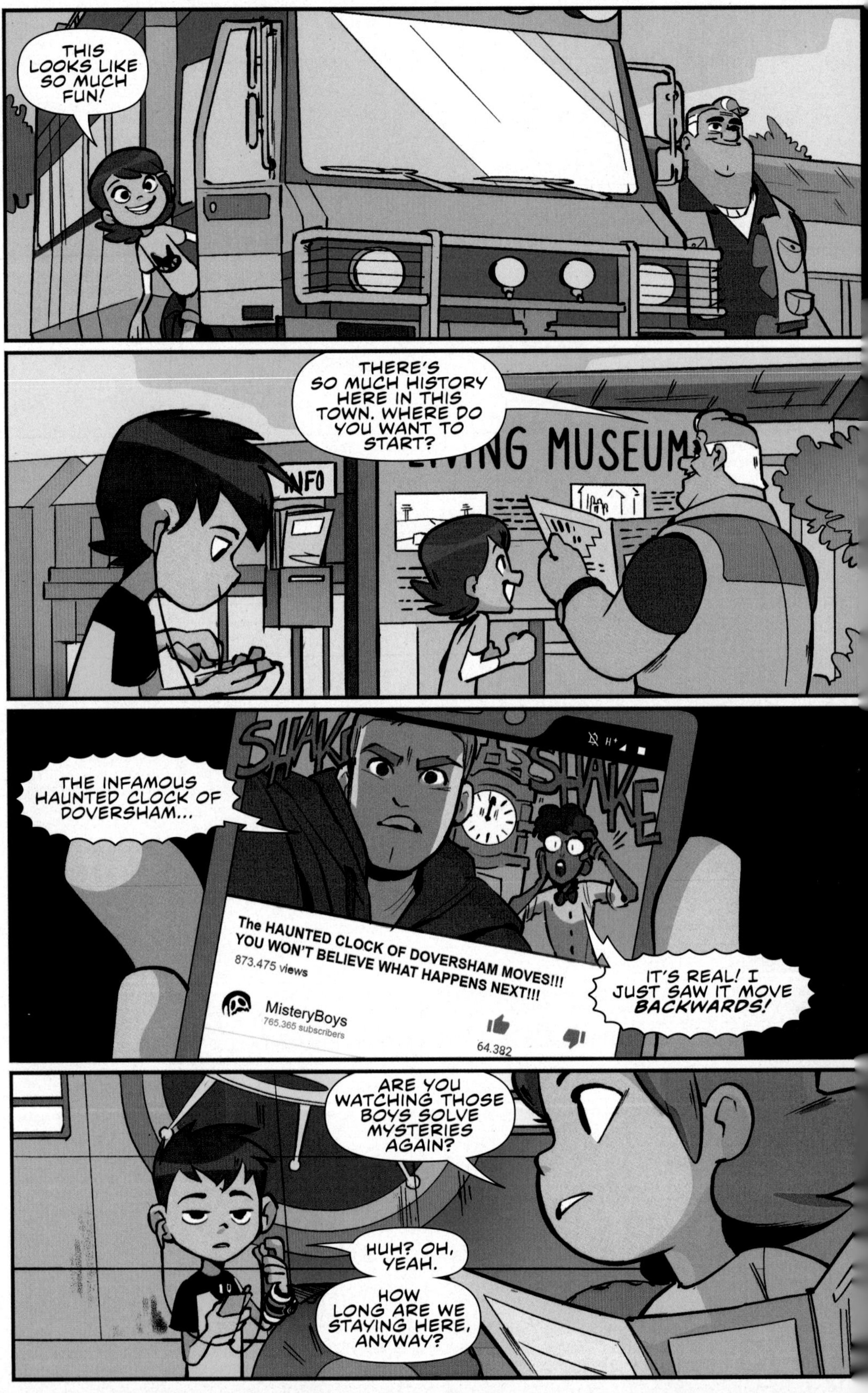
THIS LOOKS LIKE SO MUCH FUN!
THERE'S SO MUCH HISTORY HERE IN THIS TOWN. WHERE DO YOU WANT TO START?
INFO
MUSEUM
THE INFAMOUS HAUNTED CLOCK OF DOVERSHAM...
SHAKE
The HAUNTED CLOCK OF DOVERSHAM MOVES!!!
YOU WON'T BELIEVE WHAT HAPPENS NEXT!!!
873.475 views
MisteryBoys
765.365 subscribers
64.382
IT'S REAL! I JUST SAW IT MOVE *BACKWARDS!*
ARE YOU WATCHING THOSE BOYS SOLVE MYSTERIES AGAIN?
HUH? OH, YEAH.
HOW LONG ARE WE STAYING HERE, ANYWAY?

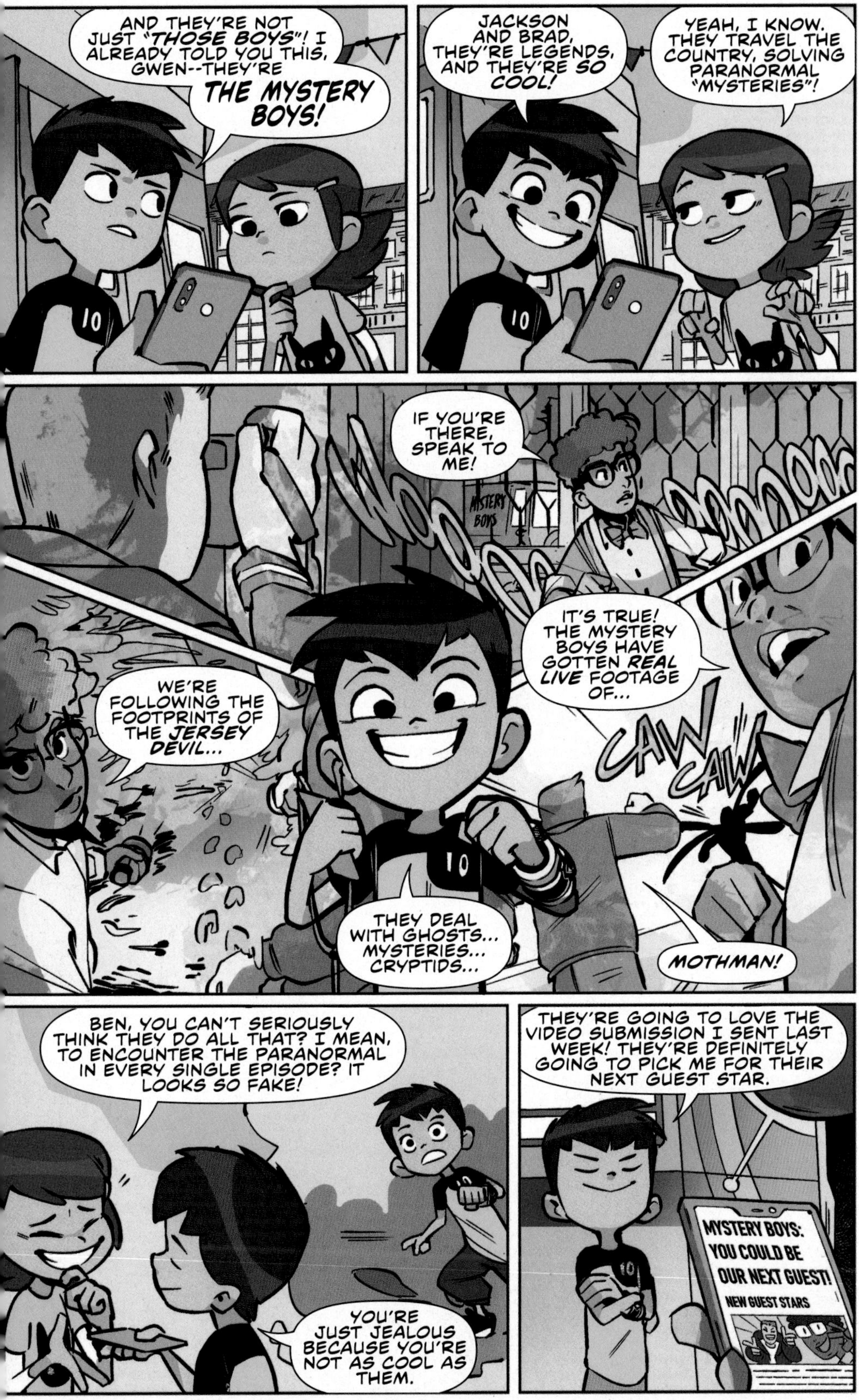
AND THEY'RE NOT JUST "THOSE BOYS"! I ALREADY TOLD YOU THIS, GWEN--THEY'RE
THE MYSTERY BOYS!
JACKSON AND BRAD, THEY'RE LEGENDS, AND THEY'RE SO COOL!
YEAH, I KNOW. THEY TRAVEL THE COUNTRY, SOLVING PARANORMAL "MYSTERIES"!
IF YOU'RE THERE, SPEAK TO ME!
MYSTERY BOYS
IT'S TRUE! THE MYSTERY BOYS HAVE GOTTEN REAL LIVE FOOTAGE OF...
WE'RE FOLLOWING THE FOOTPRINTS OF THE JERSEY DEVIL...
CAW
CAW
THEY DEAL WITH GHOSTS... MYSTERIES... CRYPTIDS...
MOTHMAN!
BEN, YOU CAN'T SERIOUSLY THINK THEY DO ALL THAT? I MEAN, TO ENCOUNTER THE PARANORMAL IN EVERY SINGLE EPISODE? IT LOOKS SO FAKE!
YOU'RE JUST JEALOUS BECAUSE YOU'RE NOT AS COOL AS THEM.
THEY'RE GOING TO LOVE THE VIDEO SUBMISSION I SENT LAST WEEK! THEY'RE DEFINITELY GOING TO PICK ME FOR THEIR NEXT GUEST STAR.
MYSTERY BOYS: YOU COULD BE OUR NEXT GUEST!
NEW GUEST STARS

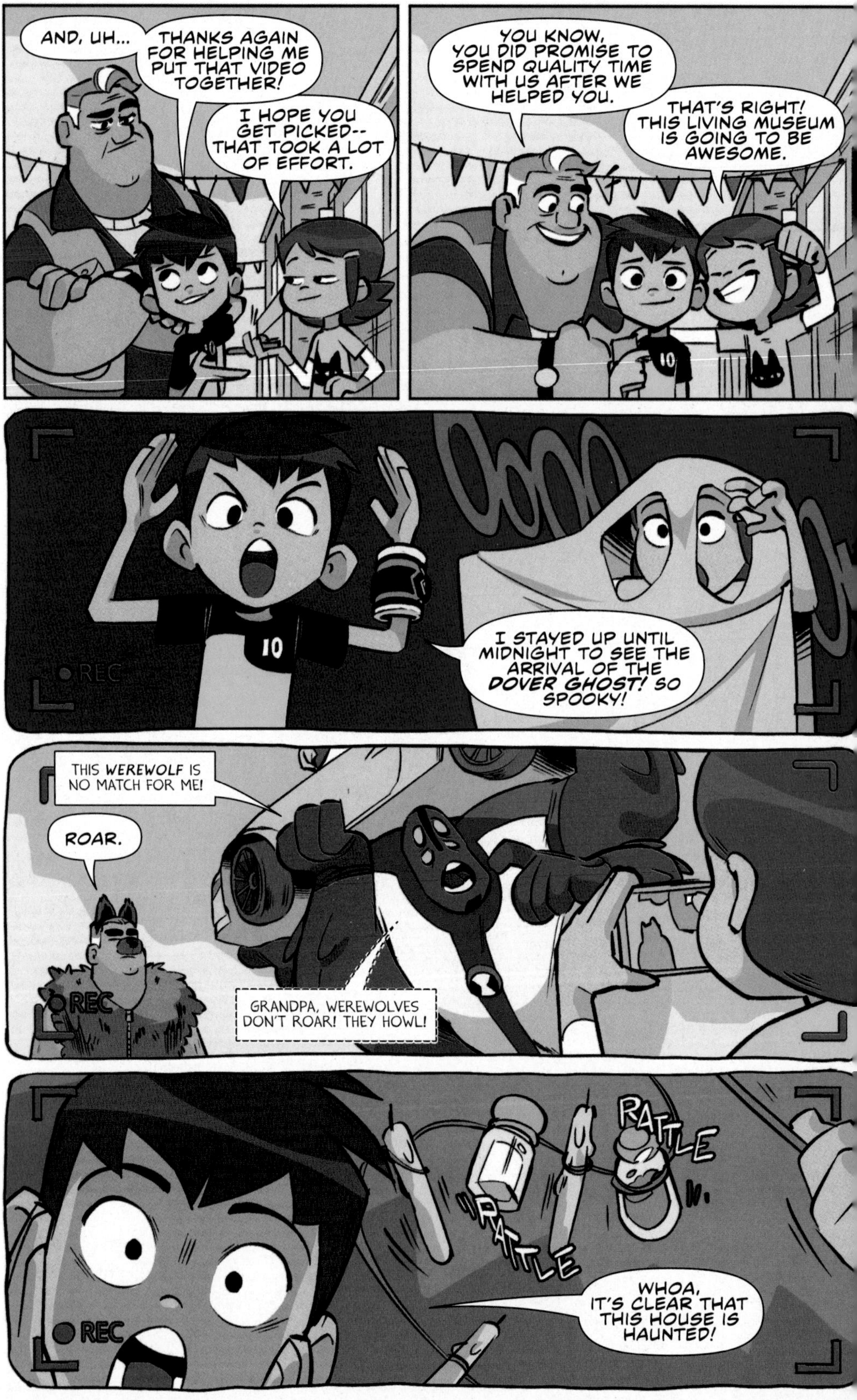
AND, UH...
THANKS AGAIN FOR HELPING ME PUT THAT VIDEO TOGETHER!
I HOPE YOU GET PICKED-- THAT TOOK A LOT OF EFFORT.
YOU KNOW, YOU DID PROMISE TO SPEND QUALITY TIME WITH US AFTER WE HELPED YOU.
THAT'S RIGHT! THIS LIVING MUSEUM IS GOING TO BE AWESOME.
REC
I STAYED UP UNTIL MIDNIGHT TO SEE THE ARRIVAL OF THE DOVER GHOST! SO SPOOKY!
THIS WEREWOLF IS NO MATCH FOR ME!
ROAR.
REC
GRANDPA, WEREWOLVES DON'T ROAR! THEY HOWL!
RATTLE
RATTLE
REC
WHOA, IT'S CLEAR THAT THIS HOUSE IS HAUNTED!

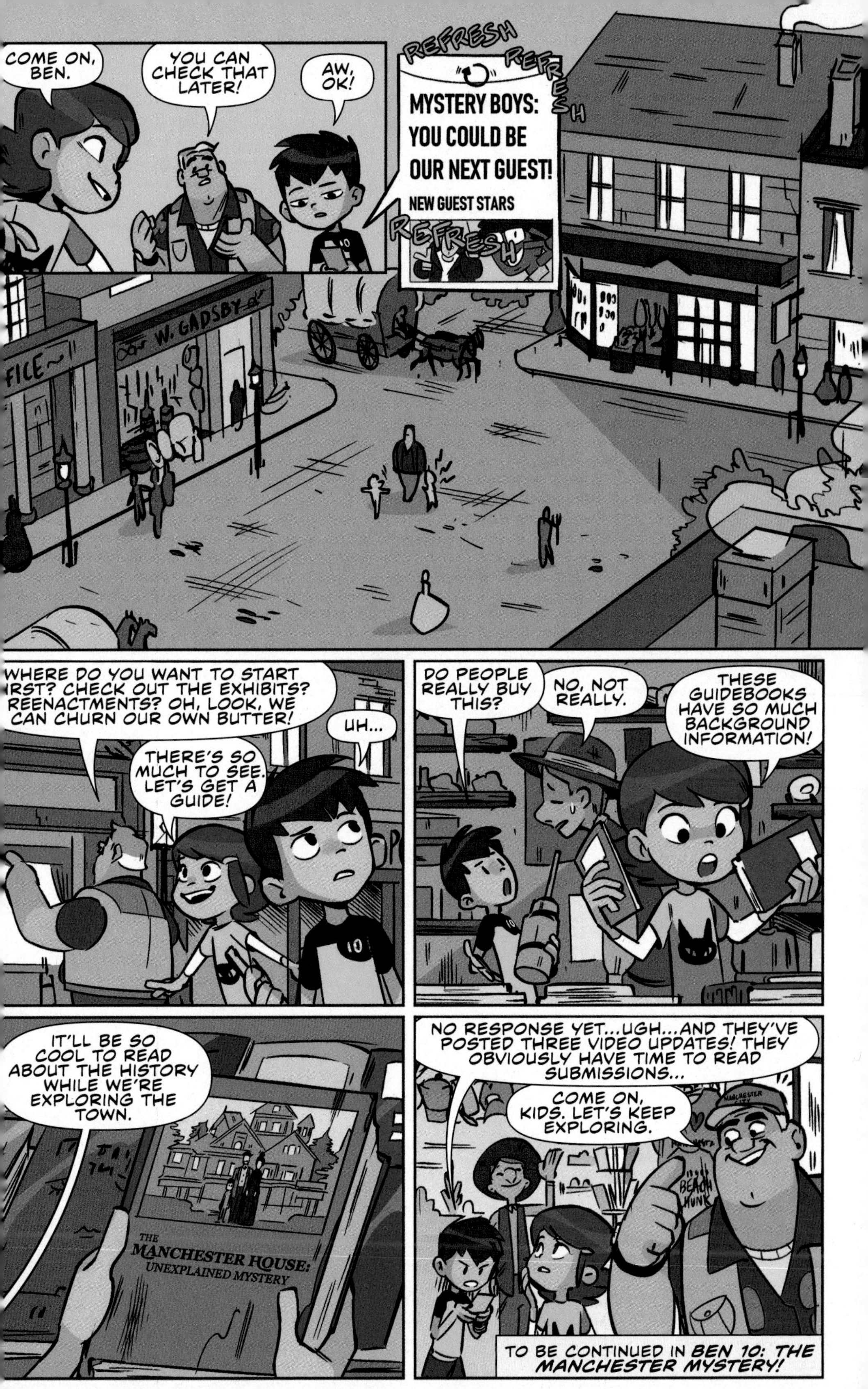

COME ON, BEN.
YOU CAN CHECK THAT LATER!
AW, OK!
REFRESH
REFRESH
MYSTERY BOYS: YOU COULD BE OUR NEXT GUEST!
NEW GUEST STARS
REFRESH
REFRESH
FICE~
W. GADSBY
WHERE DO YOU WANT TO START IRST? CHECK OUT THE EXHIBITS? REENACTMENTS? OH, LOOK, WE CAN CHURN OUR OWN BUTTER!
THERE'S SO MUCH TO SEE. LET'S GET A GUIDE!
UH...
DO PEOPLE REALLY BUY THIS?
NO, NOT REALLY.
THESE GUIDEBOOKS HAVE SO MUCH BACKGROUND INFORMATION!
IT'LL BE SO COOL TO READ ABOUT THE HISTORY WHILE WE'RE EXPLORING THE TOWN.
THE MANCHESTER HOUSE: UNEXPLAINED MYSTERY
NO RESPONSE YET...UGH...AND THEY'VE POSTED THREE VIDEO UPDATES! THEY OBVIOUSLY HAVE TIME TO READ SUBMISSIONS...
COME ON, KIDS. LET'S KEEP EXPLORING.
BEACH HUNK
TO BE CONTINUED IN *BEN 10: THE MANCHESTER MYSTERY!*

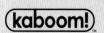